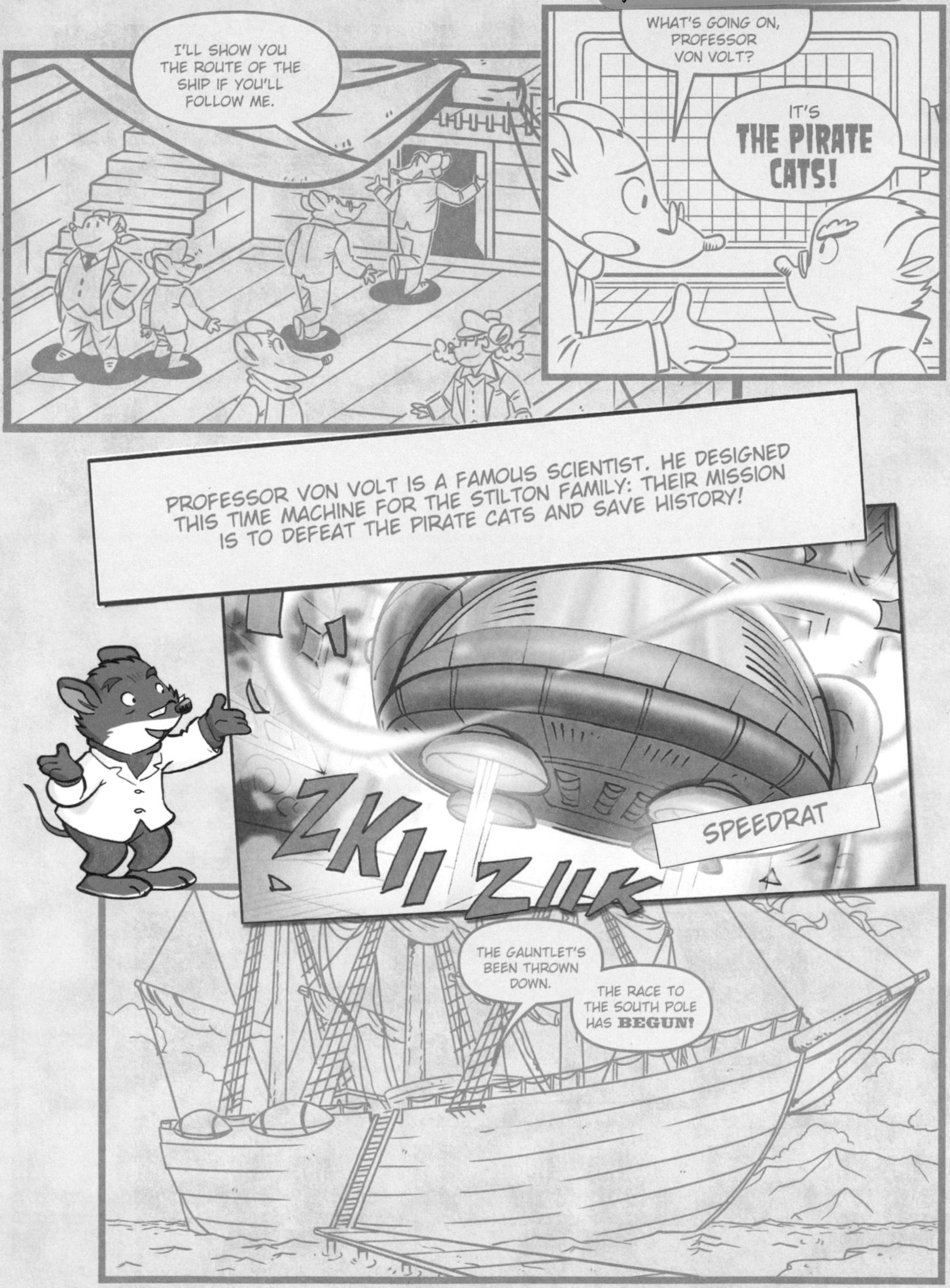
I'LL SHOW YOU THE ROUTE OF THE SHIP IF YOU'LL FOLLOW ME.
WHAT'S GOING ON, PROFESSOR VON VOLT?
IT'S THE PIRATE CATS!
PROFESSOR VON VOLT IS A FAMOUS SCIENTIST. HE DESIGNED THIS TIME MACHINE FOR THE STILTON FAMILY: THEIR MISSION IS TO DEFEAT THE PIRATE CATS AND SAVE HISTORY!
ZKII ZIIK
SPEEDRAT
THE GAUNTLET'S BEEN THROWN DOWN.
THE RACE TO THE SOUTH POLE HAS BEGUN!

Geronimo Stilton

PAPERCUTZ™

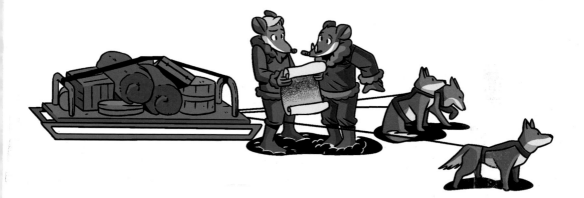

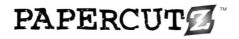

Geronimo Stilton & Thea Stilton

GRAPHIC NOVELS AVAILABLE FROM PAPERCUTZ

...ALSO AVAILABLE WHEREVER E-BOOKS ARE SOLD!

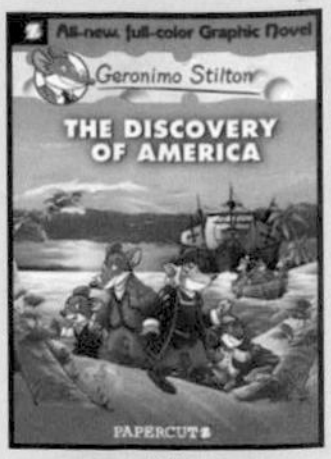
All-new, full-color Graphic Novel
Geronimo Stilton
THE DISCOVERY OF AMERICA
PAPERCUTZ

#1
"The Discovery of America"

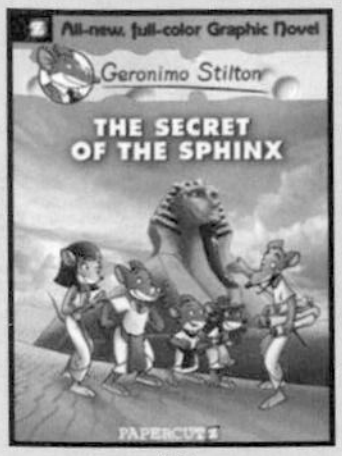
All-new, full-color Graphic Novel
Geronimo Stilton
THE SECRET OF THE SPHINX
PAPERCUTZ

#2
"The Secret of the Sphinx"

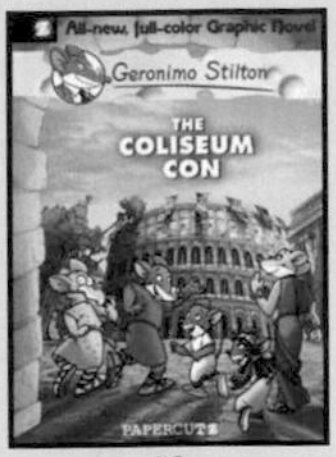
All-new, full-color Graphic Novel
Geronimo Stilton
THE COLISEUM CON
PAPERCUTZ

#3
"The Coliseum Con"

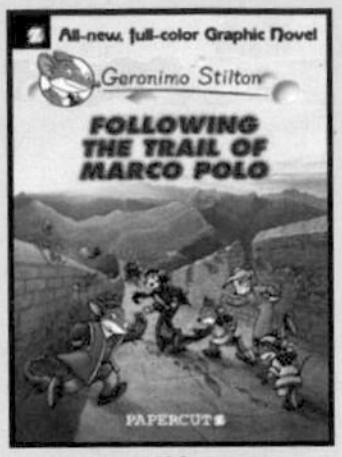
All-new, full-color Graphic Novel
Geronimo Stilton
FOLLOWING THE TRAIL OF MARCO POLO
PAPERCUTZ

#4
"Following the Trail of Marco Polo"

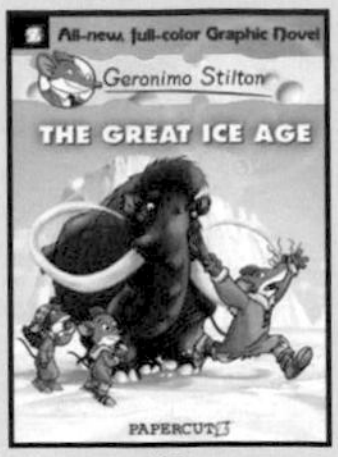
All-new, full-color Graphic Novel
Geronimo Stilton
THE GREAT ICE AGE
PAPERCUTZ

#5
"The Great Ice Age"

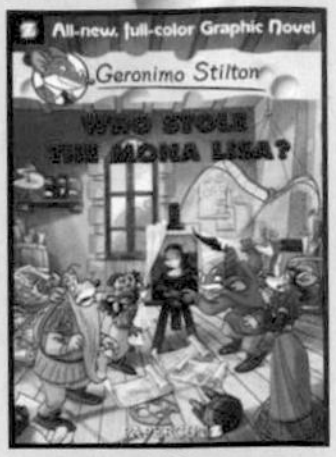
All-new, full-color Graphic Novel
Geronimo Stilton
WHO STOLE THE MONA LISA?

#6
"Who Stole The Mona Lisa?"

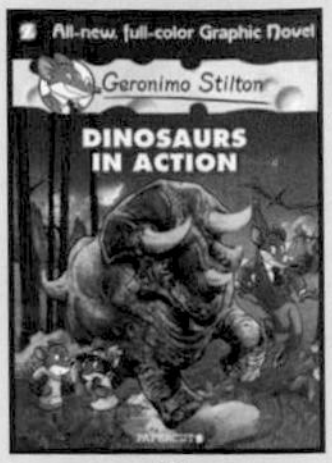
All-new, full-color Graphic Novel
Geronimo Stilton
DINOSAURS IN ACTION

#7
"Dinosaurs in Action"

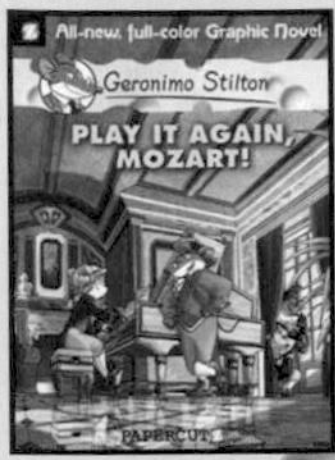
All-new, full-color Graphic Novel
Geronimo Stilton
PLAY IT AGAIN, MOZART!

#8
"Play It Again, Mozart!"

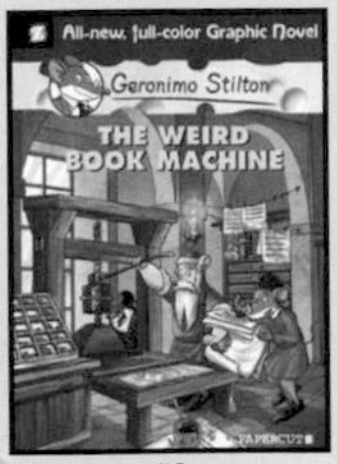
All-new, full-color Graphic Novel
Geronimo Stilton
THE WEIRD BOOK MACHINE

#9
"The Weird Book Machine"

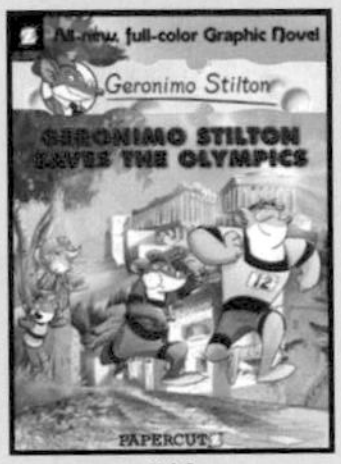
All-new, full-color Graphic Novel
Geronimo Stilton
GERONIMO STILTON SAVES THE OLYMPICS
PAPERCUTZ

#10
"Geronimo Stilton Saves the Olympics"

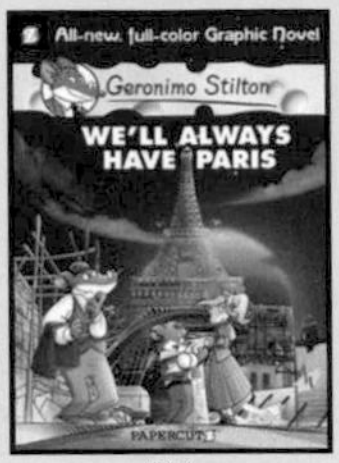
All-new, full-color Graphic Novel
Geronimo Stilton
WE'LL ALWAYS HAVE PARIS
PAPERCUTZ

#11
"We'll Always Have Paris"

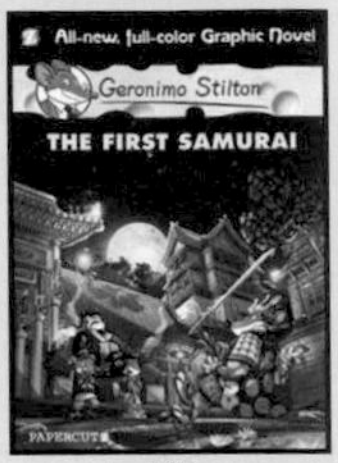
All-new, full-color Graphic Novel
Geronimo Stilton
THE FIRST SAMURAI
PAPERCUTZ

#12
"The First Samurai"

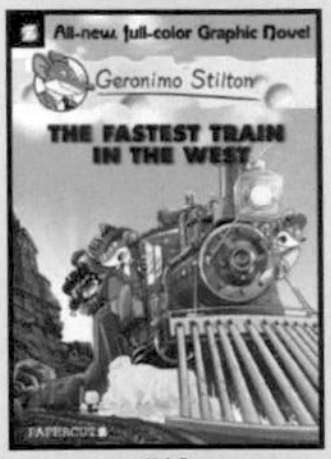
All-new, full-color Graphic Novel
Geronimo Stilton
THE FASTEST TRAIN IN THE WEST
PAPERCUTZ

#13
"The Fastest Train in the West"

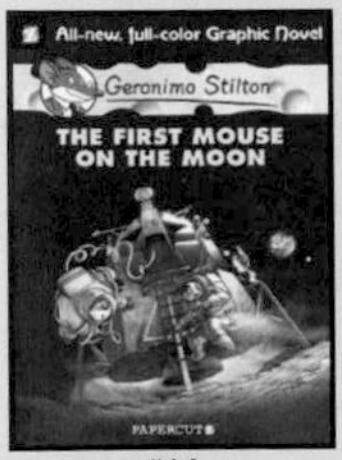
All-new, full-color Graphic Novel
Geronimo Stilton
THE FIRST MOUSE ON THE MOON
PAPERCUTZ

#14
"The First Mouse on the Moon"

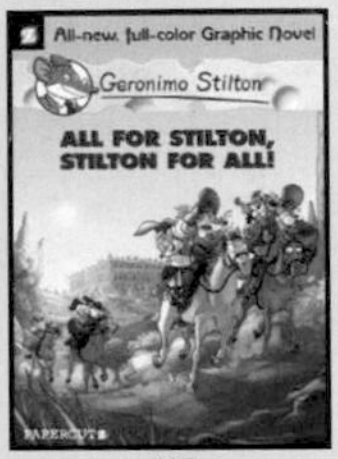
All-new, full-color Graphic Novel
Geronimo Stilton
ALL FOR STILTON, STILTON FOR ALL!
PAPERCUTZ

#15
"All for Stilton, Stilton for All!"

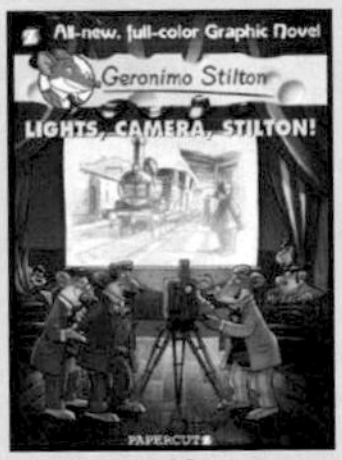
All-new, full-color Graphic Novel
Geronimo Stilton
LIGHTS, CAMERA, STILTON!
PAPERCUTZ

#16
"Lights, Camera, Stilton!"

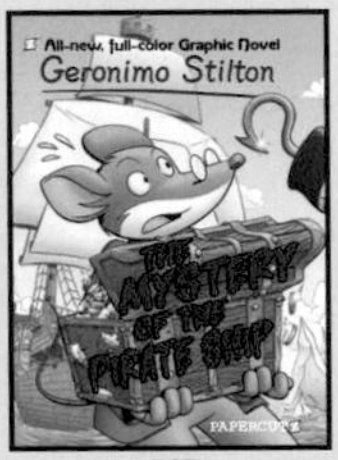
All-new, full-color Graphic Novel
Geronimo Stilton
THE MYSTERY OF THE PIRATE SHIP
PAPERCUTZ

#17
"The Mystery of the Pirate Ship"

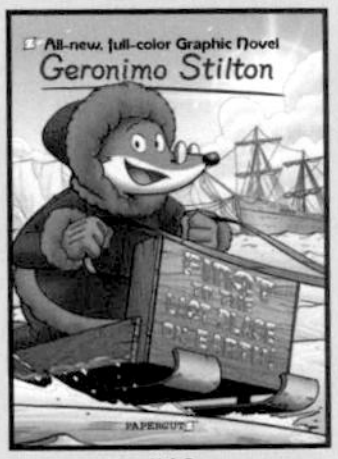
All-new, full-color Graphic Novel
Geronimo Stilton
PAPERCUTZ

#18
"First to the Last Place on Earth!"

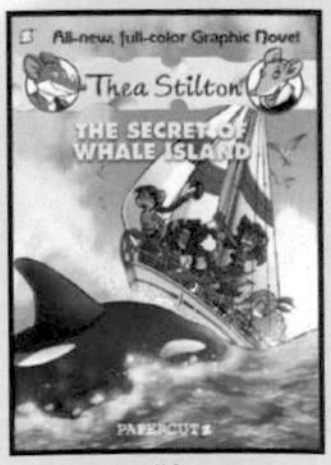
All-new, full-color Graphic Novel
Thea Stilton
THE SECRET OF WHALE ISLAND
PAPERCUTZ

#1
"The Secret of Whale Island"

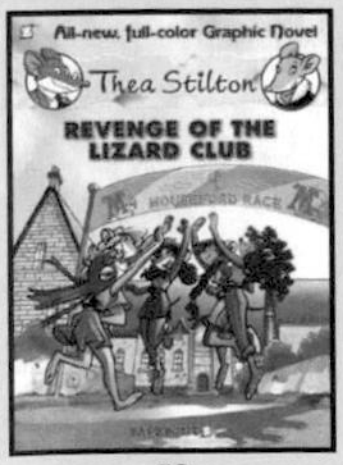
All-new, full-color Graphic Novel
Thea Stilton
REVENGE OF THE LIZARD CLUB

#2
"Revenge of the Lizard Club"

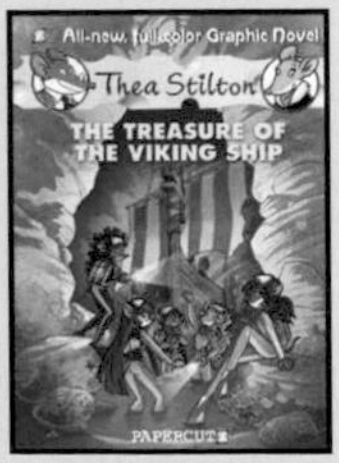
All-new, full-color Graphic Novel
Thea Stilton
THE TREASURE OF THE VIKING SHIP
PAPERCUTZ

#3
"The Treasure of the Viking Ship"

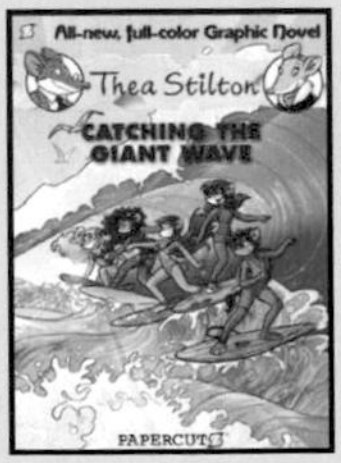
All-new, full-color Graphic Novel
Thea Stilton
CATCHING THE GIANT WAVE
PAPERCUTZ

#4
"Catching the Giant Wave"

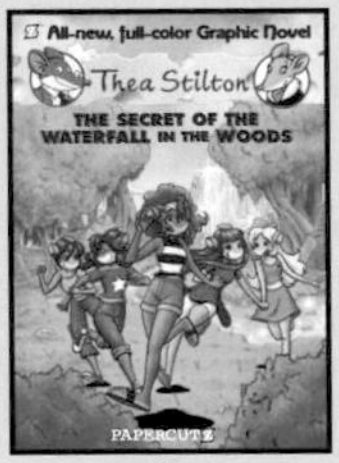
All-new, full-color Graphic Novel
Thea Stilton
THE SECRET OF THE WATERFALL IN THE WOODS
PAPERCUTZ

#5
"The Secret of the Waterfall in the Woods"

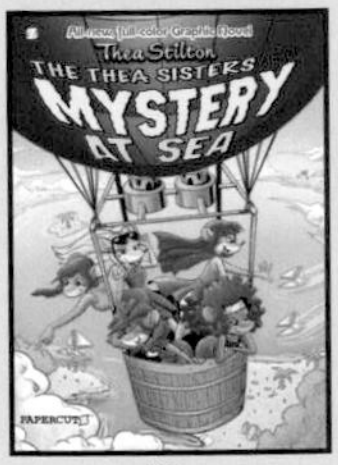
All-new, full-color Graphic Novel
Thea Stilton
THE THEA SISTERS
MYSTERY AT SEA
PAPERCUTZ

#6
"The Thea Sisters and the Mystery at Sea"

papercutz.com

GERONIMO STILTON and THEA STILTON graphic novels are available for $9.99 each only in hardcover. Available from booksellers everywhere. You can also order online from papercutz.com. Or call 1-800-886-1223, Monday through Friday, 9 – 5 EST. MC, Visa, and AmEx accepted. To order by mail, please add $4.00 for postage and handling for first book ordered, $1.00 for each additional book and make check payable to NBM Publishing.
Send to: Papercutz, 160 Broadway, Suite 700, East Wing, New York, NY 10038.

Geronimo Stilton

FIRST TO THE LAST PLACE ON EARTH!

By Geronimo Stilton

PAPERCUTZ™

NEW YORK

GERONIMO STILTON #18
FIRST TO THE LAST PLACE ON EARTH!
Geronimo Stilton names, characters and related indicia are copyright, trademark, and exclusive license of Atlantyca S.p.A.
All rights reserved.
The moral right of the author has been asserted.

Text by Geronimo Stilton
Cover by Ryan Jampole (art) and JayJay Jackson (color)
Editorial supervision by Alessandra Berello and Margherita Banal (Atlantyca S.p.A.)
Script by Francesco Savino and Leonardo Favia
Translation by Nanette McGuinness
Art by Ryan Jampole
Color by Laurie E. Smith and JayJay Jackson
Lettering by Wilson Ramos Jr.

© Atlantyca S.p.A. – via Leopardi 8, 20123 Milano, Italia – foreignrights@atlantyca.it
© 2016 for this Work in English language by Papercutz, 160 Broadway, Suite 700, East Wing, New York, NY 10038

Based on an original idea by Elisabetta Dami

www.geronimostilton.com

Stilton is the name of a famous English cheese. It is a registered trademark of the Stilton Cheese Makers' Association.
For more information go to www.stiltoncheese.com

Papercutz books may be purchased for business or promotional use.
For information on bulk purchases, please contact Macmillan Corporate and Premium Sales Department at (800) 221-7945 x5442.

Production – Dawn Guzzo
Production Coordinator – Jeff Whitman
Assistant Managing Editor – Jeff Whitman
Jim Salicrup
Editor-in-Chief

ISBN: 978-1-62991-603-3

Printed in China
November 2016 by WKT Co. LTD.

Distributed by Macmillan
First Printing

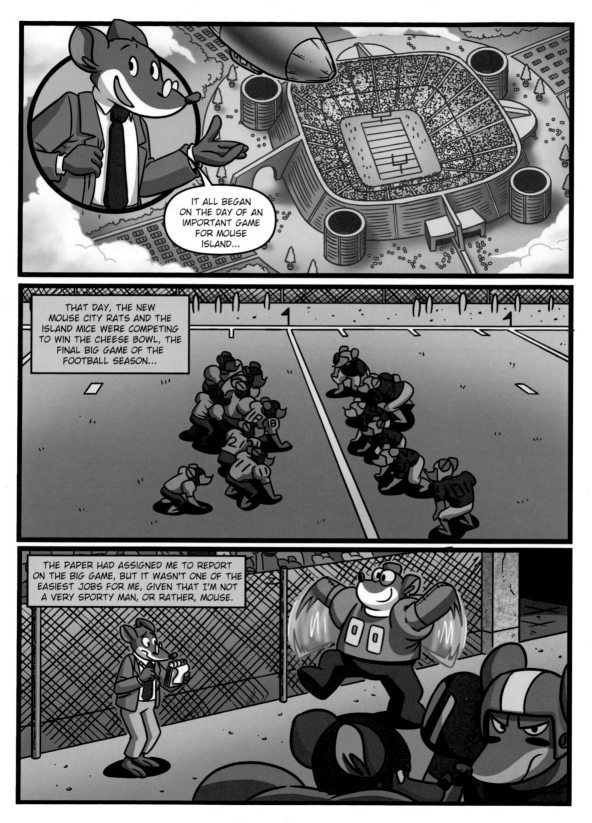

IT ALL BEGAN ON THE DAY OF AN IMPORTANT GAME FOR MOUSE ISLAND...

THAT DAY, THE NEW MOUSE CITY RATS AND THE ISLAND MICE WERE COMPETING TO WIN THE CHEESE BOWL, THE FINAL BIG GAME OF THE FOOTBALL SEASON...

THE PAPER HAD ASSIGNED ME TO REPORT ON THE BIG GAME, BUT IT WASN'T ONE OF THE EASIEST JOBS FOR ME, GIVEN THAT I'M NOT A VERY SPORTY MAN, OR RATHER, MOUSE.

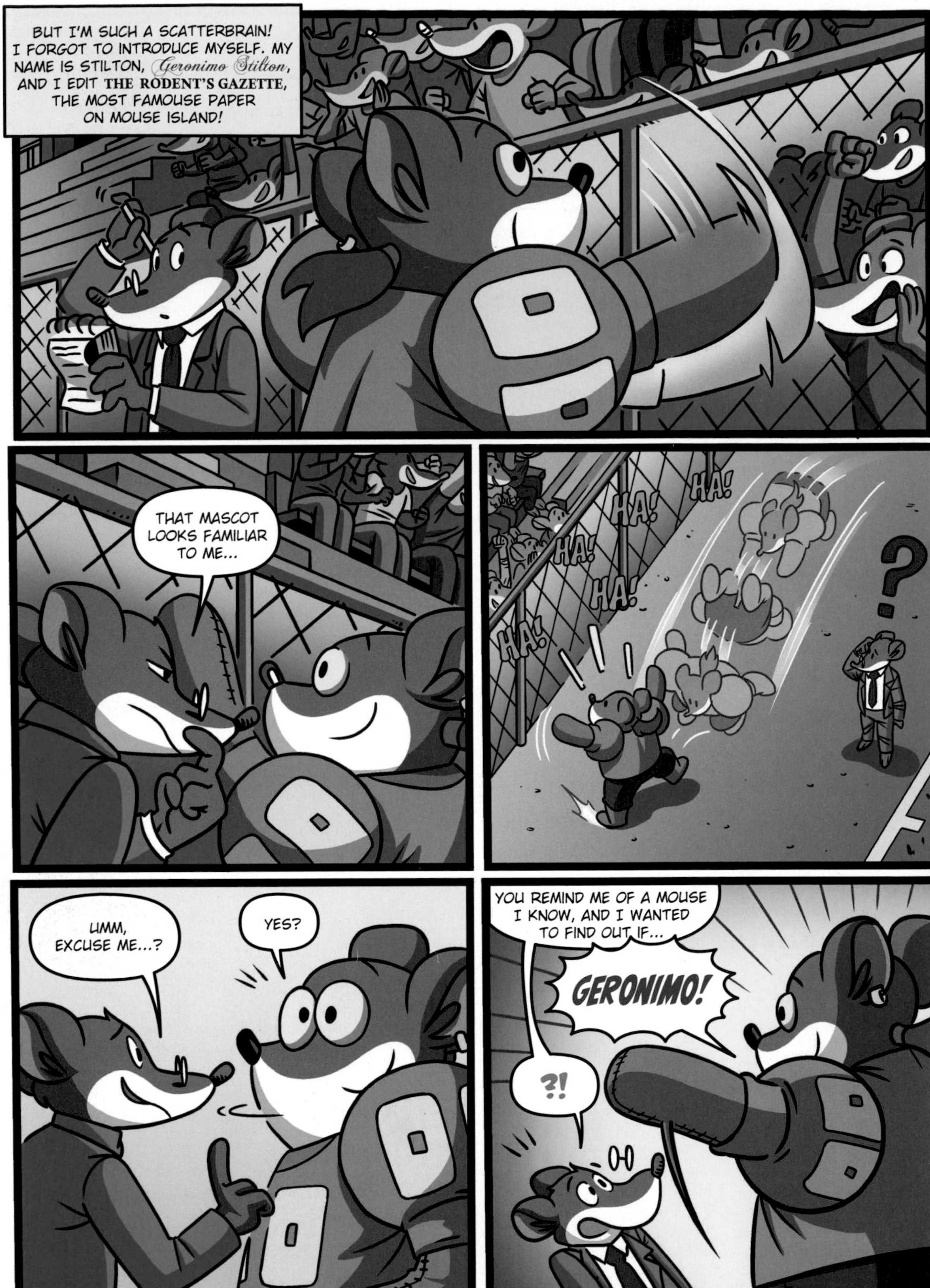
BUT I'M SUCH A SCATTERBRAIN! I FORGOT TO INTRODUCE MYSELF. MY NAME IS STILTON, *Geronimo Stilton*, AND I EDIT THE RODENT'S GAZETTE, THE MOST FAMOUSE PAPER ON MOUSE ISLAND!
THAT MASCOT LOOKS FAMILIAR TO ME...
HA!
HA!
HA!
HA!
HA!
?
UMM, EXCUSE ME...?
YES?
YOU REMIND ME OF A MOUSE I KNOW, AND I WANTED TO FIND OUT IF...
GERONIMO!
?!

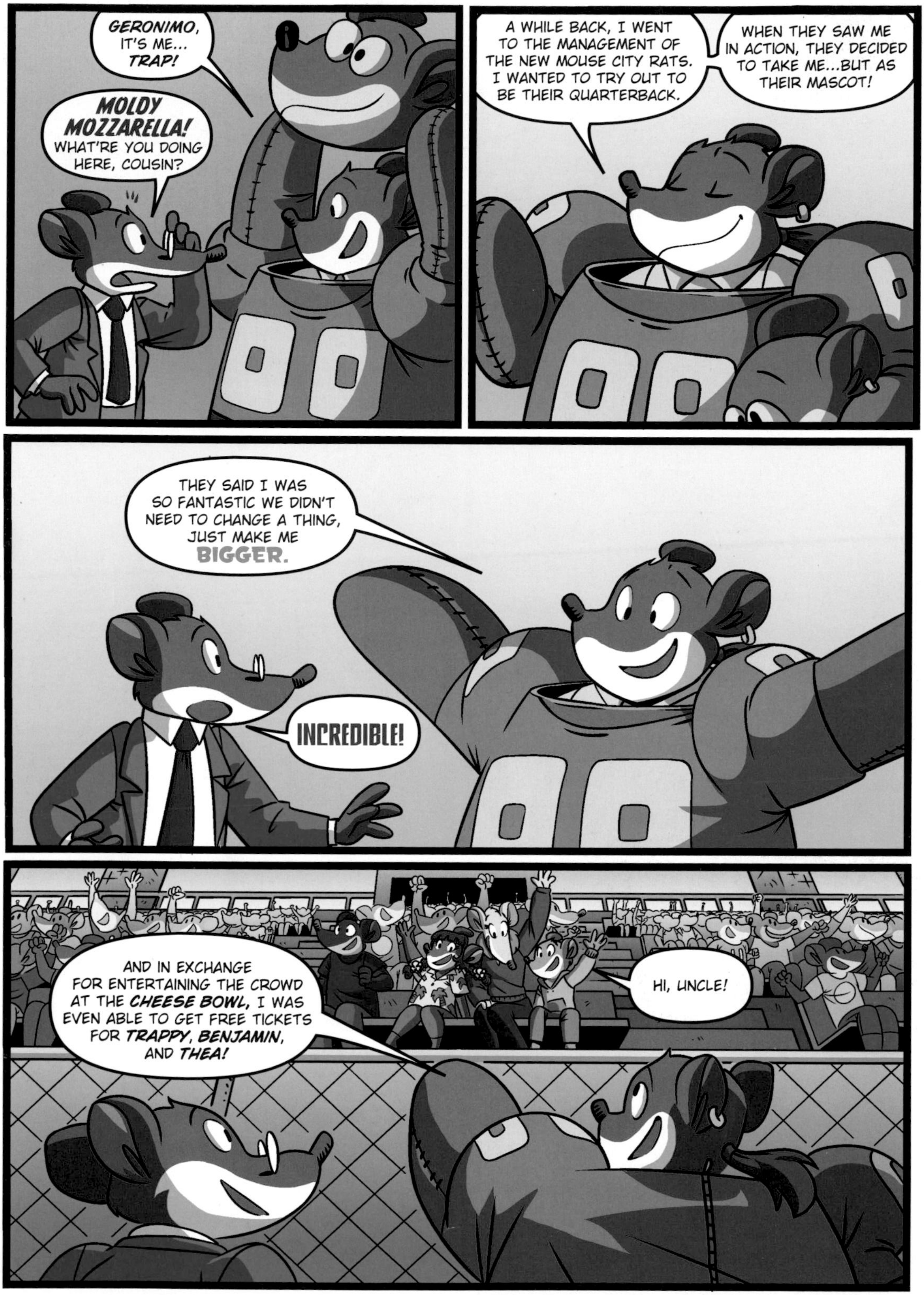
GERONIMO, IT'S ME... TRAP!
MOLDY MOZZARELLA! WHAT'RE YOU DOING HERE, COUSIN?
A WHILE BACK, I WENT TO THE MANAGEMENT OF THE NEW MOUSE CITY RATS. I WANTED TO TRY OUT TO BE THEIR QUARTERBACK.
WHEN THEY SAW ME IN ACTION, THEY DECIDED TO TAKE ME...BUT AS THEIR MASCOT!
THEY SAID I WAS SO FANTASTIC WE DIDN'T NEED TO CHANGE A THING, JUST MAKE ME BIGGER.
INCREDIBLE!
AND IN EXCHANGE FOR ENTERTAINING THE CROWD AT THE CHEESE BOWL, I WAS EVEN ABLE TO GET FREE TICKETS FOR TRAPPY, BENJAMIN, AND THEA!
HI, UNCLE!

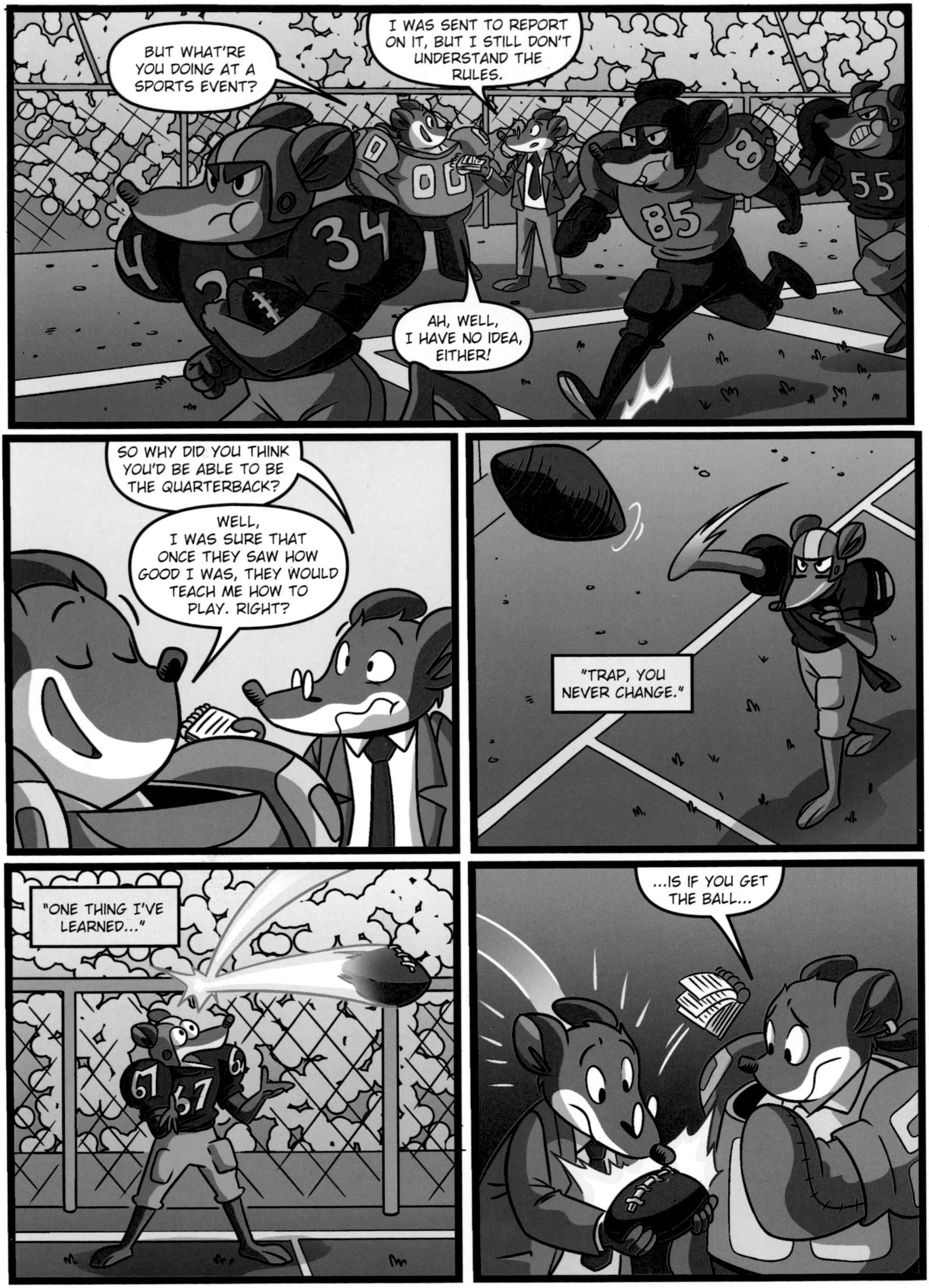
BUT WHAT'RE YOU DOING AT A SPORTS EVENT?
I WAS SENT TO REPORT ON IT, BUT I STILL DON'T UNDERSTAND THE RULES.
AH, WELL, I HAVE NO IDEA, EITHER!
SO WHY DID YOU THINK YOU'D BE ABLE TO BE THE QUARTERBACK?
WELL, I WAS SURE THAT ONCE THEY SAW HOW GOOD I WAS, THEY WOULD TEACH ME HOW TO PLAY. RIGHT?
"TRAP, YOU NEVER CHANGE."
"ONE THING I'VE LEARNED..."
...IS IF YOU GET THE BALL...

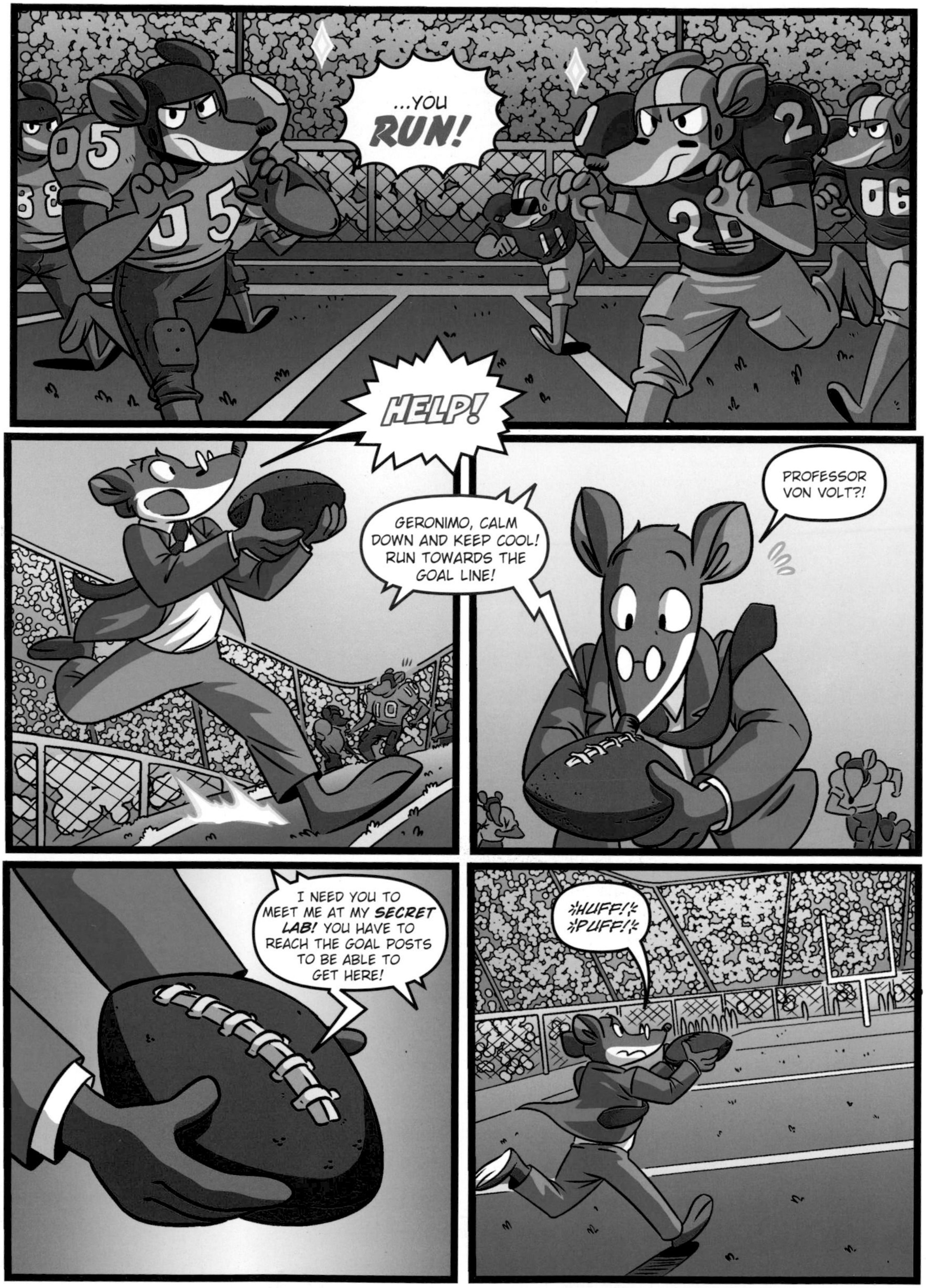
...YOU RUN!
HELP!
GERONIMO, CALM DOWN AND KEEP COOL! RUN TOWARDS THE GOAL LINE!
PROFESSOR VON VOLT?!
I NEED YOU TO MEET ME AT MY SECRET LAB! YOU HAVE TO REACH THE GOAL POSTS TO BE ABLE TO GET HERE!
HUFF! PUFF!

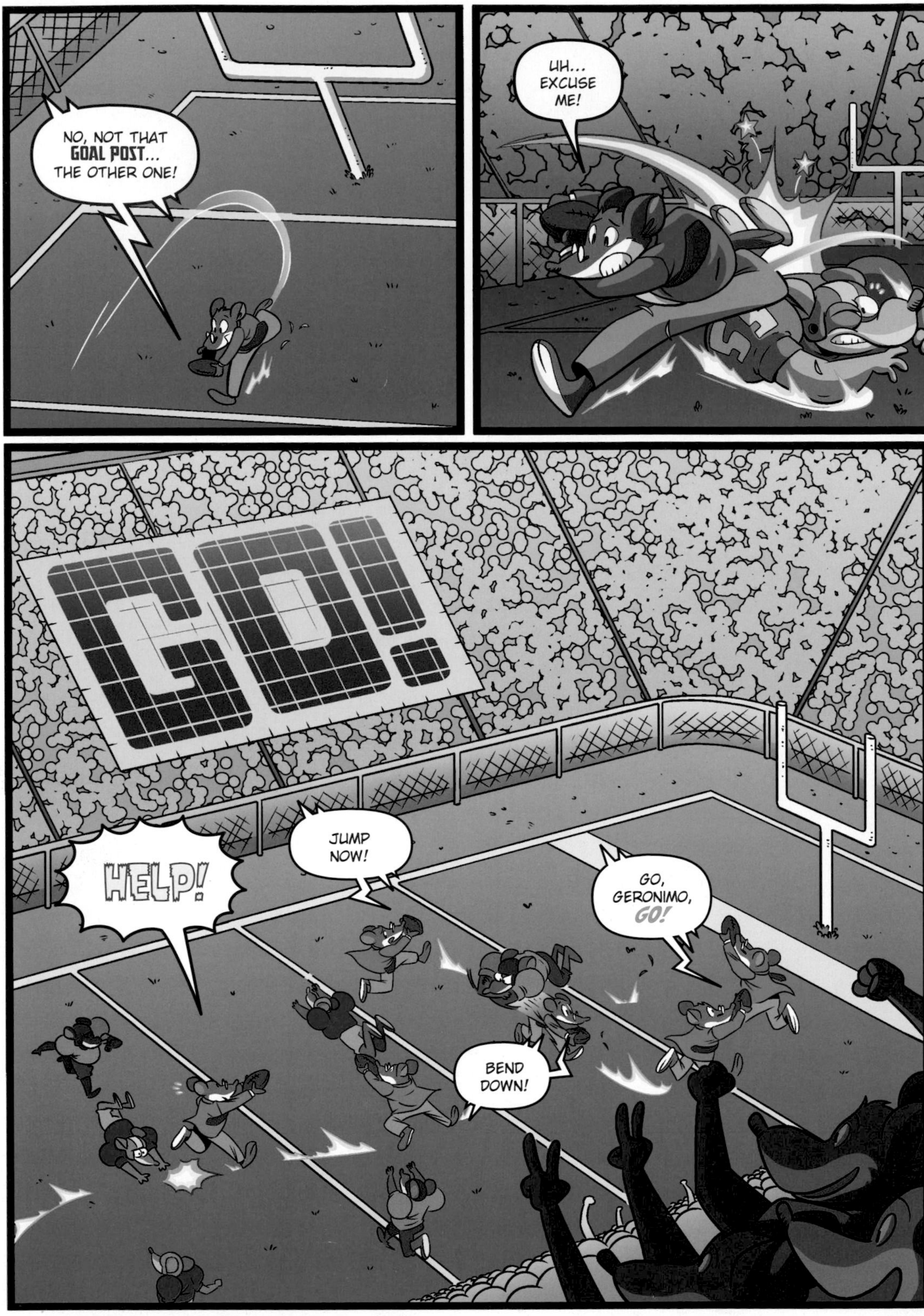
NO, NOT THAT GOAL POST... THE OTHER ONE!
UH... EXCUSE ME!
GO!
HELP!
JUMP NOW!
GO, GERONIMO, GO!
BEND DOWN!

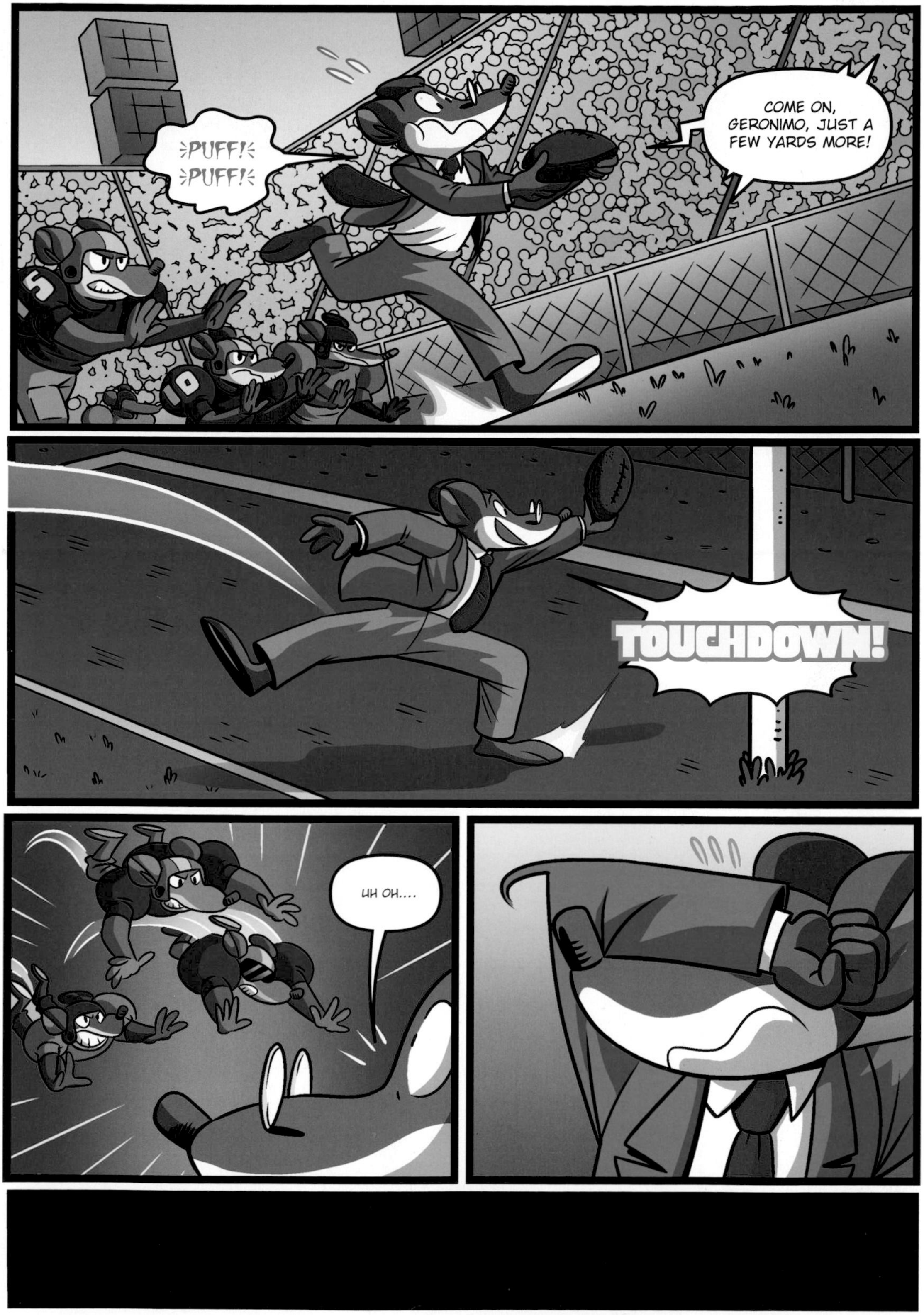
PUFF!
PUFF!
COME ON, GERONIMO, JUST A FEW YARDS MORE!
TOUCHDOWN!
UH OH....

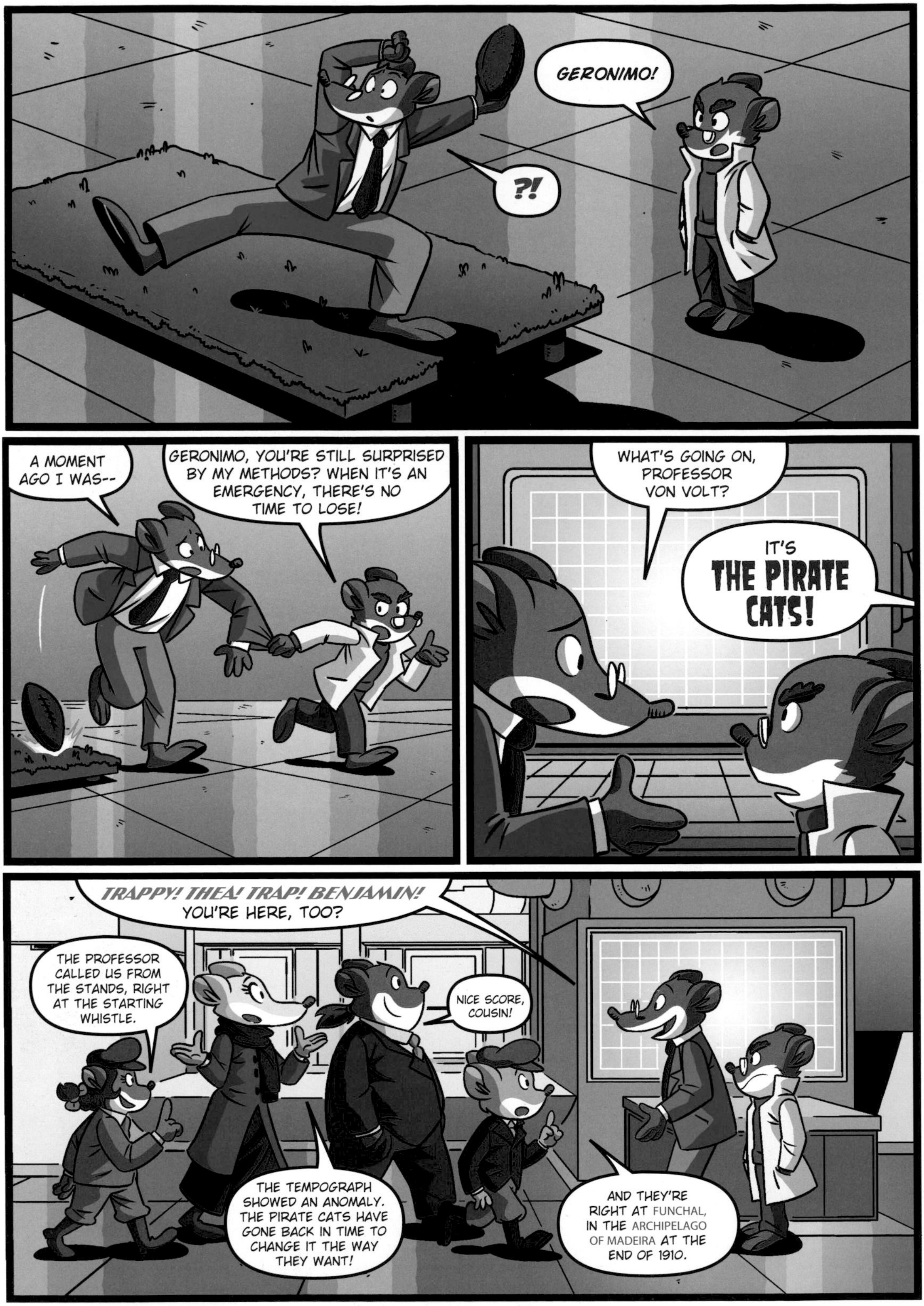
GERONIMO!
?!
A MOMENT AGO I WAS--
GERONIMO, YOU'RE STILL SURPRISED BY MY METHODS? WHEN IT'S AN EMERGENCY, THERE'S NO TIME TO LOSE!
WHAT'S GOING ON, PROFESSOR VON VOLT?
IT'S THE PIRATE CATS!
TRAPPY! THEA! TRAP! BENJAMIN! YOU'RE HERE, TOO?
THE PROFESSOR CALLED US FROM THE STANDS, RIGHT AT THE STARTING WHISTLE.
THE TEMPOGRAPH SHOWED AN ANOMALY. THE PIRATE CATS HAVE GONE BACK IN TIME TO CHANGE IT THE WAY THEY WANT!
NICE SCORE, COUSIN!
AND THEY'RE RIGHT AT FUNCHAL, IN THE ARCHIPELAGO OF MADEIRA AT THE END OF 1910.

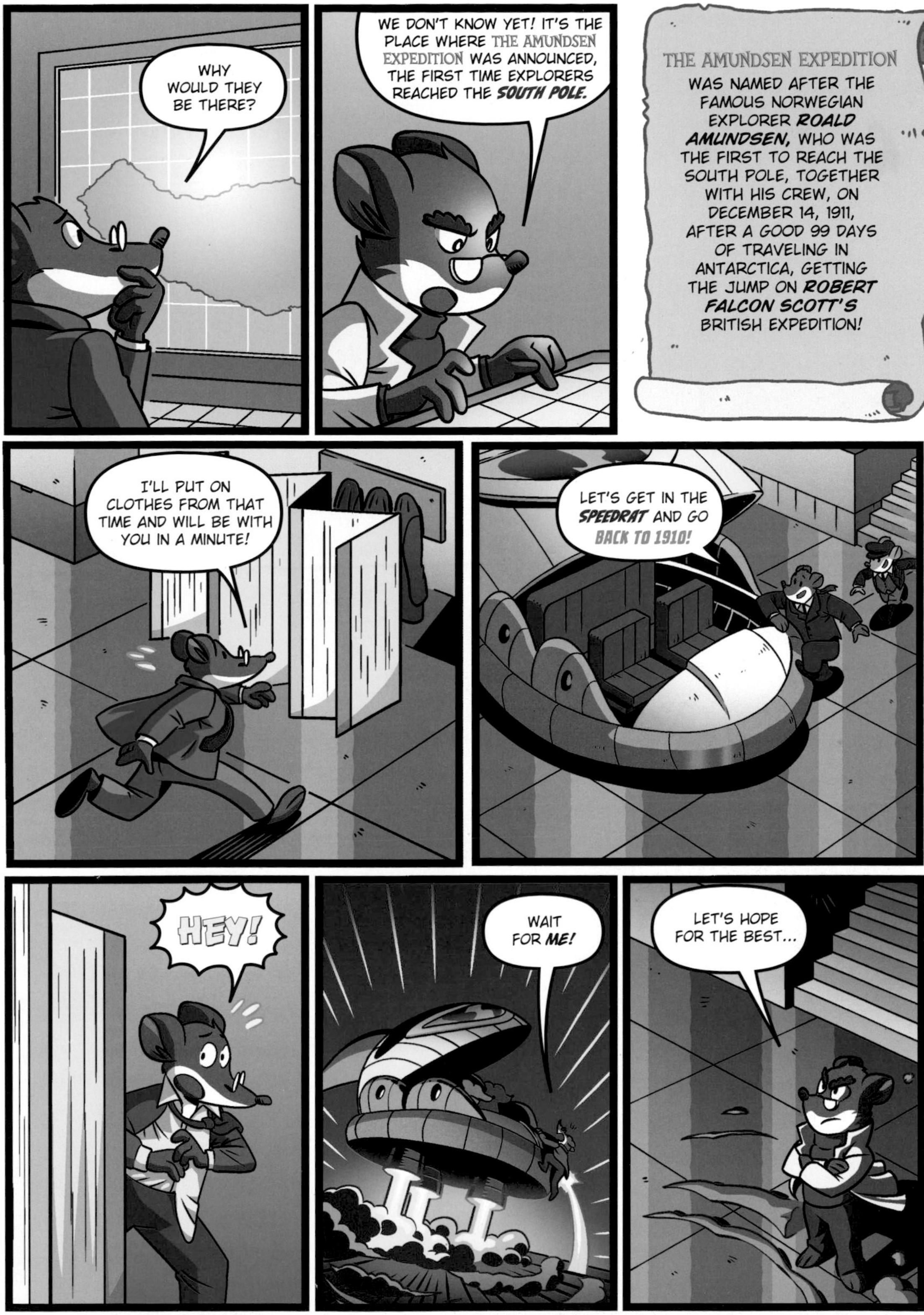
WHY WOULD THEY BE THERE?
WE DON'T KNOW YET! IT'S THE PLACE WHERE THE AMUNDSEN EXPEDITION WAS ANNOUNCED, THE FIRST TIME EXPLORERS REACHED THE SOUTH POLE.
THE AMUNDSEN EXPEDITION
WAS NAMED AFTER THE FAMOUS NORWEGIAN EXPLORER ROALD AMUNDSEN, WHO WAS THE FIRST TO REACH THE SOUTH POLE, TOGETHER WITH HIS CREW, ON DECEMBER 14, 1911, AFTER A GOOD 99 DAYS OF TRAVELING IN ANTARCTICA, GETTING THE JUMP ON ROBERT FALCON SCOTT'S BRITISH EXPEDITION!
I'LL PUT ON CLOTHES FROM THAT TIME AND WILL BE WITH YOU IN A MINUTE!
LET'S GET IN THE SPEEDRAT AND GO BACK TO 1910!
HEY!
WAIT FOR ME!
LET'S HOPE FOR THE BEST...

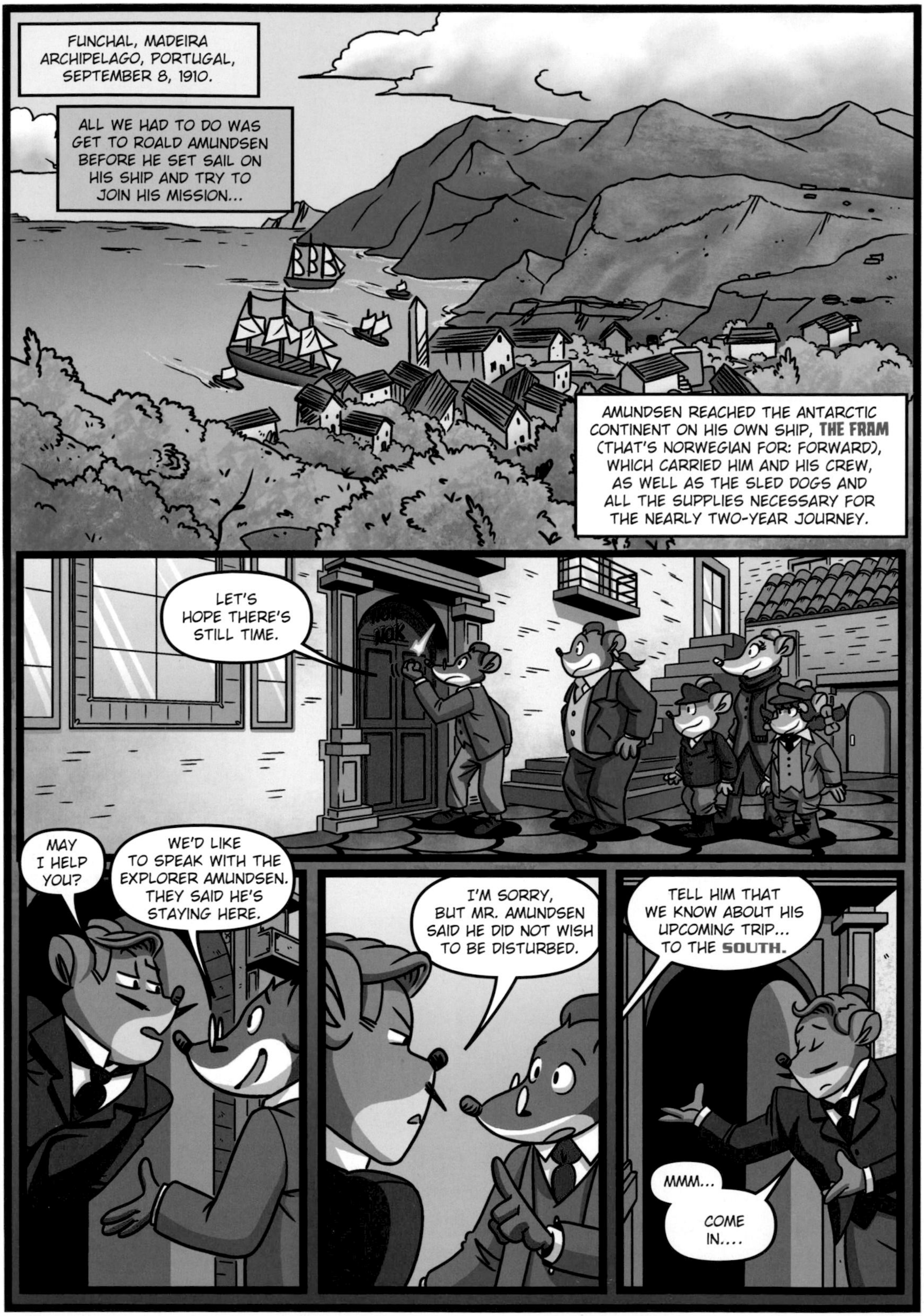
FUNCHAL, MADEIRA ARCHIPELAGO, PORTUGAL, SEPTEMBER 8, 1910.
ALL WE HAD TO DO WAS GET TO ROALD AMUNDSEN BEFORE HE SET SAIL ON HIS SHIP AND TRY TO JOIN HIS MISSION...
AMUNDSEN REACHED THE ANTARCTIC CONTINENT ON HIS OWN SHIP, THE FRAM (THAT'S NORWEGIAN FOR: FORWARD), WHICH CARRIED HIM AND HIS CREW, AS WELL AS THE SLED DOGS AND ALL THE SUPPLIES NECESSARY FOR THE NEARLY TWO-YEAR JOURNEY.
LET'S HOPE THERE'S STILL TIME.
MAY I HELP YOU?
WE'D LIKE TO SPEAK WITH THE EXPLORER AMUNDSEN. THEY SAID HE'S STAYING HERE.
I'M SORRY, BUT MR. AMUNDSEN SAID HE DID NOT WISH TO BE DISTURBED.
TELL HIM THAT WE KNOW ABOUT HIS UPCOMING TRIP... TO THE SOUTH.
MMM...
COME IN....

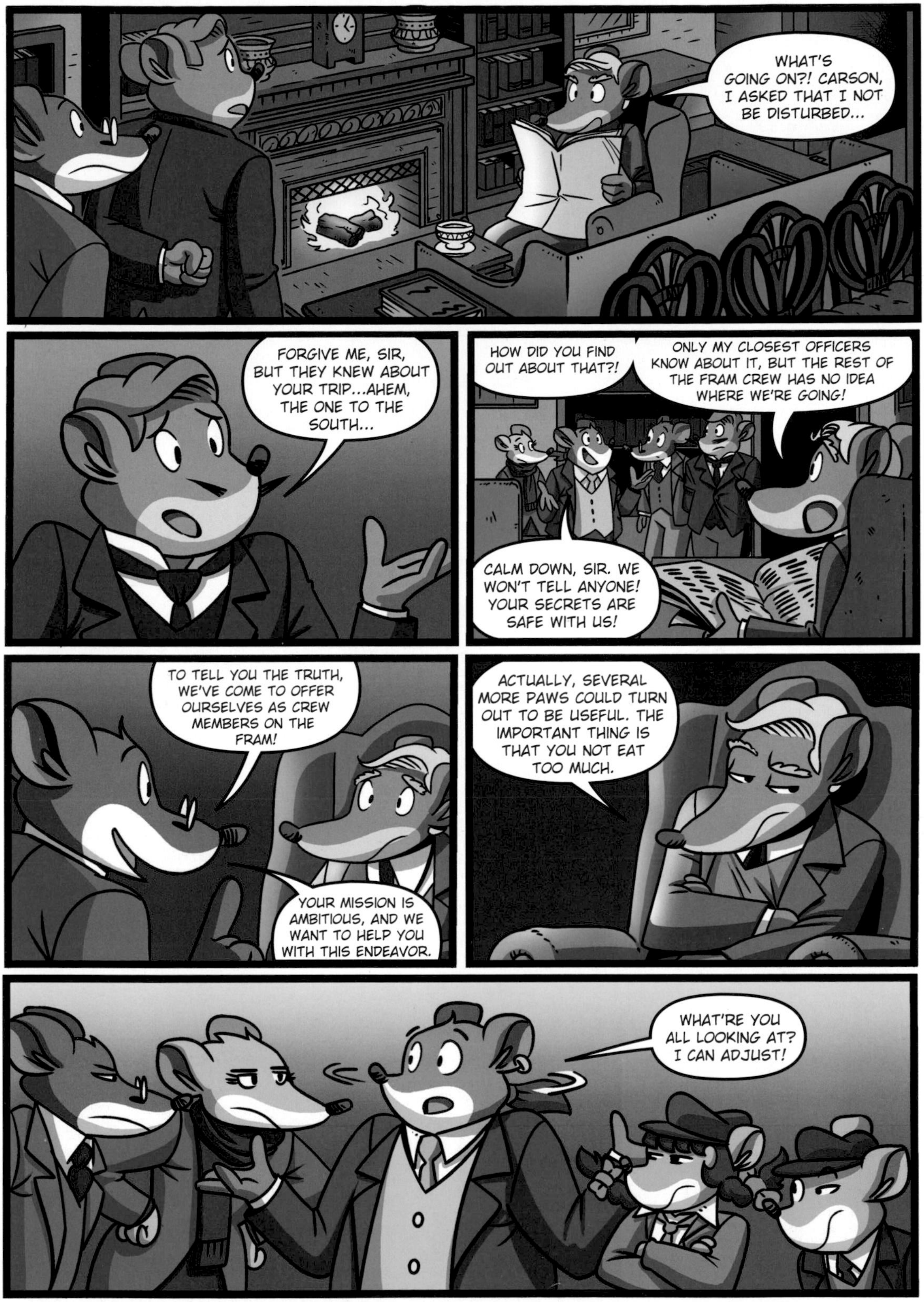

WHAT'S GOING ON?! CARSON, I ASKED THAT I NOT BE DISTURBED...
FORGIVE ME, SIR, BUT THEY KNEW ABOUT YOUR TRIP...AHEM, THE ONE TO THE SOUTH...
HOW DID YOU FIND OUT ABOUT THAT?!
ONLY MY CLOSEST OFFICERS KNOW ABOUT IT, BUT THE REST OF THE FRAM CREW HAS NO IDEA WHERE WE'RE GOING!
CALM DOWN, SIR. WE WON'T TELL ANYONE! YOUR SECRETS ARE SAFE WITH US!
TO TELL YOU THE TRUTH, WE'VE COME TO OFFER OURSELVES AS CREW MEMBERS ON THE FRAM!
YOUR MISSION IS AMBITIOUS, AND WE WANT TO HELP YOU WITH THIS ENDEAVOR.
ACTUALLY, SEVERAL MORE PAWS COULD TURN OUT TO BE USEFUL. THE IMPORTANT THING IS THAT YOU NOT EAT TOO MUCH.
WHAT'RE YOU ALL LOOKING AT? I CAN ADJUST!

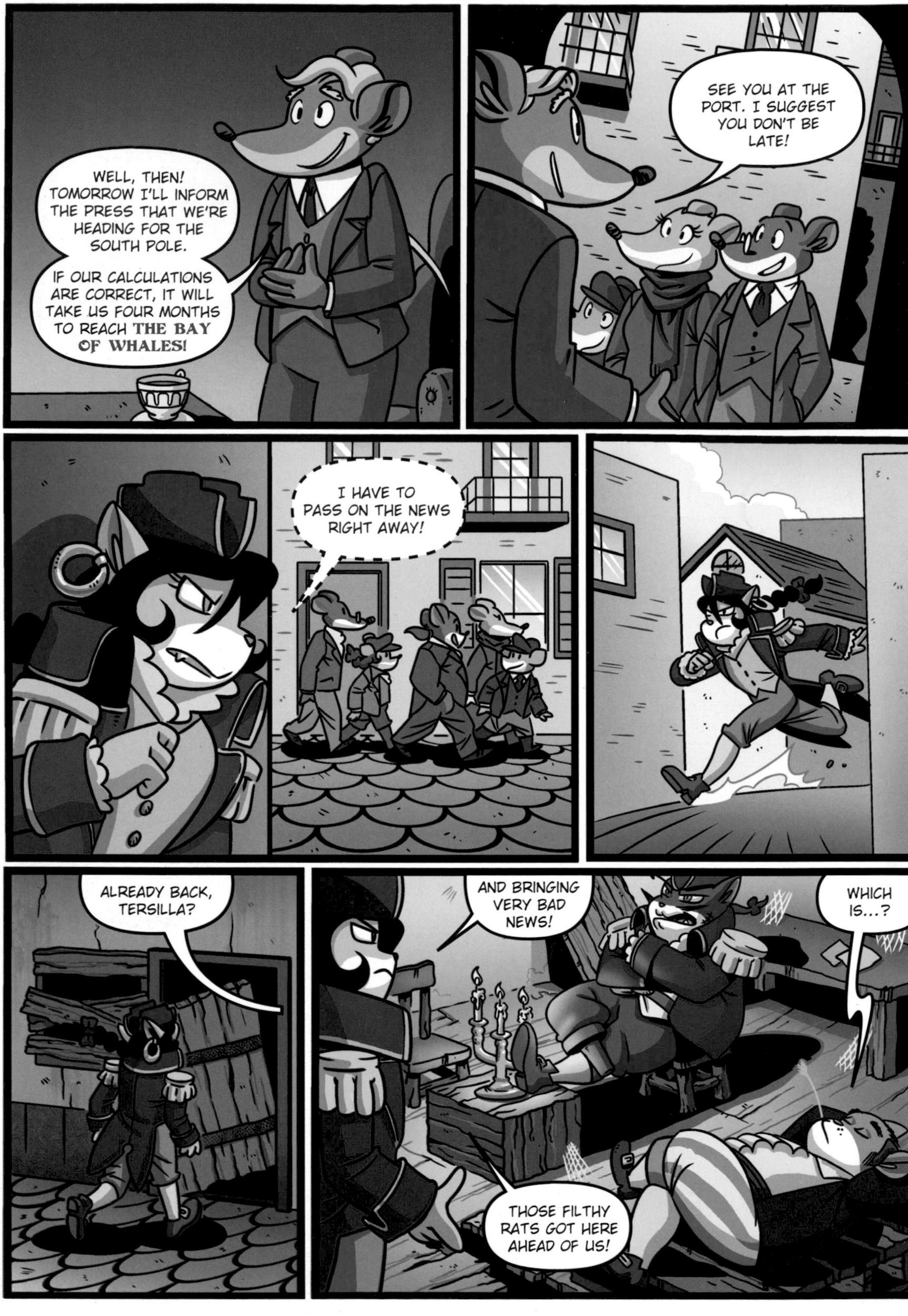
WELL, THEN! TOMORROW I'LL INFORM THE PRESS THAT WE'RE HEADING FOR THE SOUTH POLE.
IF OUR CALCULATIONS ARE CORRECT, IT WILL TAKE US FOUR MONTHS TO REACH THE BAY OF WHALES!
SEE YOU AT THE PORT. I SUGGEST YOU DON'T BE LATE!
I HAVE TO PASS ON THE NEWS RIGHT AWAY!
ALREADY BACK, TERSILLA?
AND BRINGING VERY BAD NEWS!
WHICH IS...?
THOSE FILTHY RATS GOT HERE AHEAD OF US!

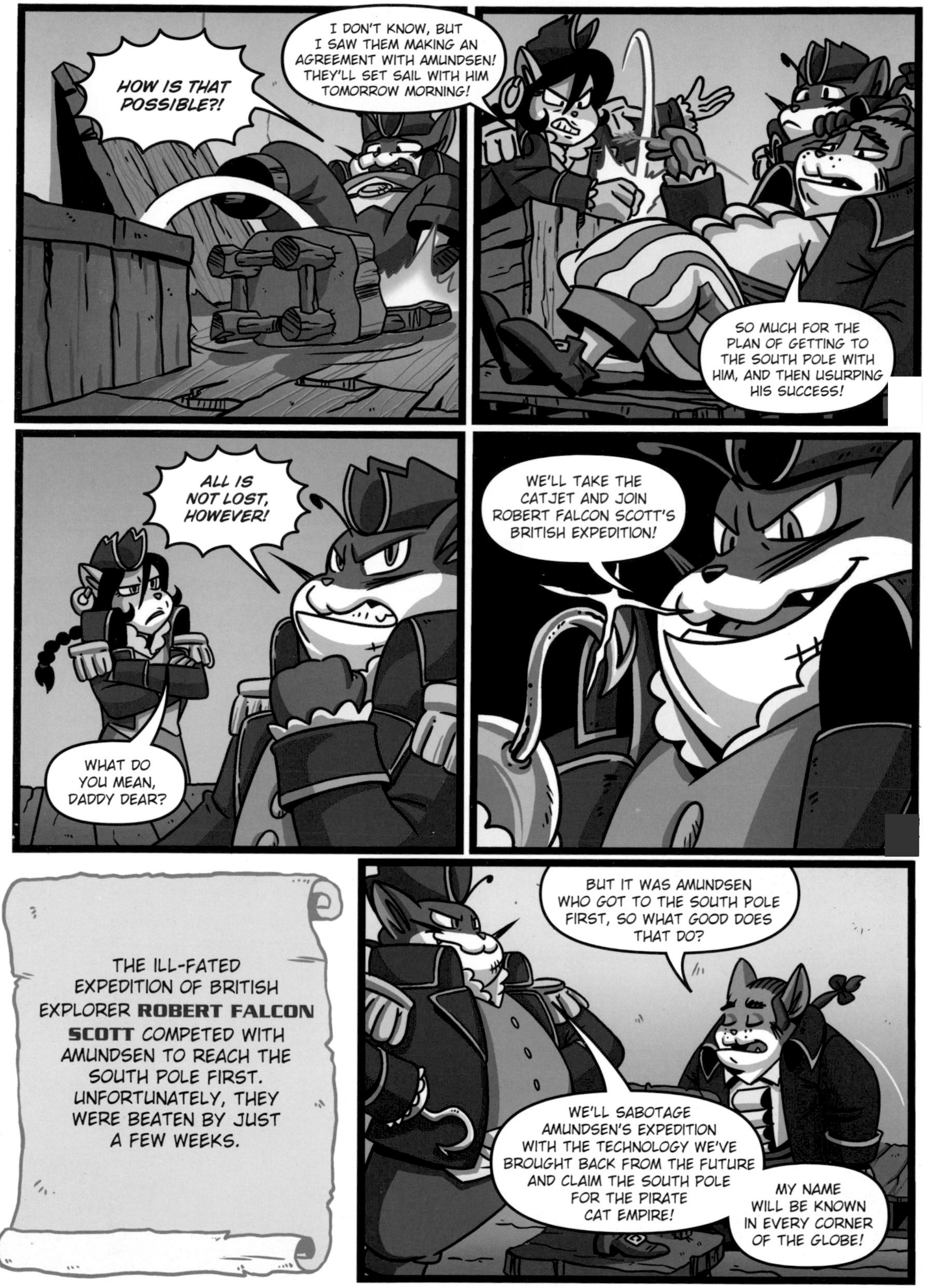
HOW IS THAT POSSIBLE?!
I DON'T KNOW, BUT I SAW THEM MAKING AN AGREEMENT WITH AMUNDSEN! THEY'LL SET SAIL WITH HIM TOMORROW MORNING!
SO MUCH FOR THE PLAN OF GETTING TO THE SOUTH POLE WITH HIM, AND THEN USURPING HIS SUCCESS!
ALL IS NOT LOST, HOWEVER!
WHAT DO YOU MEAN, DADDY DEAR?
WE'LL TAKE THE CATJET AND JOIN ROBERT FALCON SCOTT'S BRITISH EXPEDITION!
THE ILL-FATED EXPEDITION OF BRITISH EXPLORER **ROBERT FALCON SCOTT** COMPETED WITH AMUNDSEN TO REACH THE SOUTH POLE FIRST. UNFORTUNATELY, THEY WERE BEATEN BY JUST A FEW WEEKS.
BUT IT WAS AMUNDSEN WHO GOT TO THE SOUTH POLE FIRST, SO WHAT GOOD DOES THAT DO?
WE'LL SABOTAGE AMUNDSEN'S EXPEDITION WITH THE TECHNOLOGY WE'VE BROUGHT BACK FROM THE FUTURE AND CLAIM THE SOUTH POLE FOR THE PIRATE CAT EMPIRE!
MY NAME WILL BE KNOWN IN EVERY CORNER OF THE GLOBE!

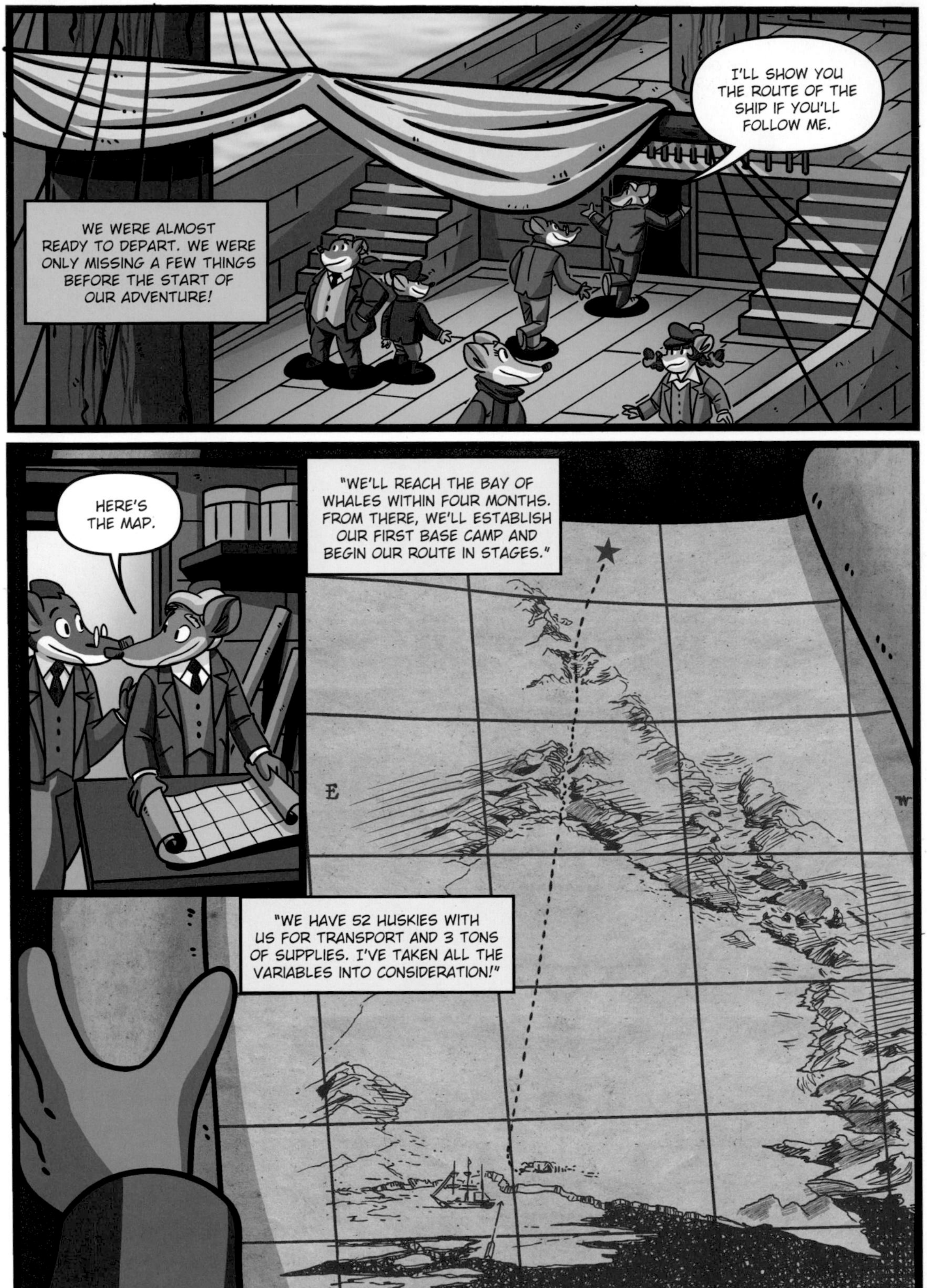
I'LL SHOW YOU THE ROUTE OF THE SHIP IF YOU'LL FOLLOW ME.
WE WERE ALMOST READY TO DEPART. WE WERE ONLY MISSING A FEW THINGS BEFORE THE START OF OUR ADVENTURE!
HERE'S THE MAP.
"WE'LL REACH THE BAY OF WHALES WITHIN FOUR MONTHS. FROM THERE, WE'LL ESTABLISH OUR FIRST BASE CAMP AND BEGIN OUR ROUTE IN STAGES."
E
W
"WE HAVE 52 HUSKIES WITH US FOR TRANSPORT AND 3 TONS OF SUPPLIES. I'VE TAKEN ALL THE VARIABLES INTO CONSIDERATION!"

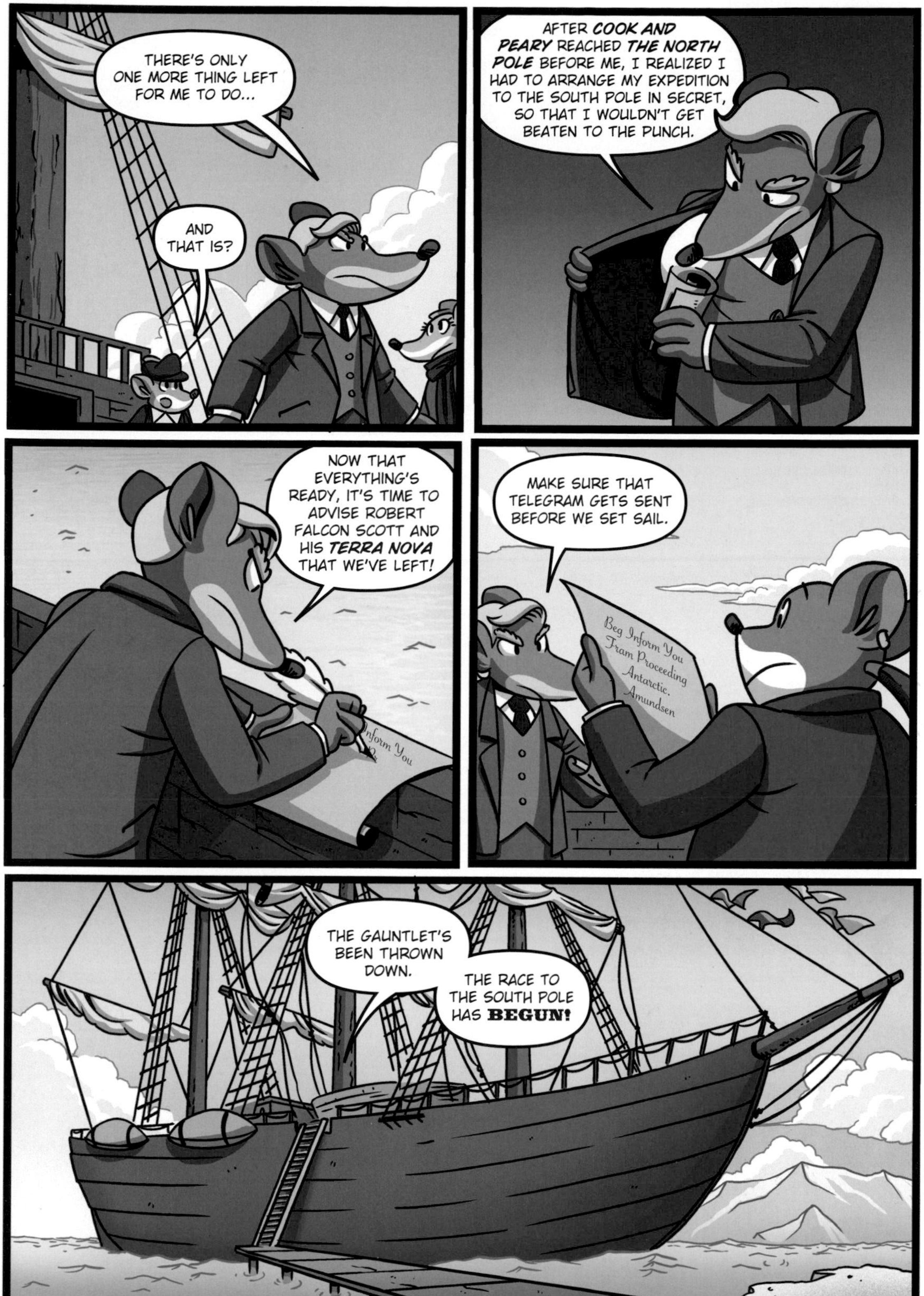
THERE'S ONLY ONE MORE THING LEFT FOR ME TO DO...
AND THAT IS?
AFTER COOK AND PEARY REACHED THE NORTH POLE BEFORE ME, I REALIZED I HAD TO ARRANGE MY EXPEDITION TO THE SOUTH POLE IN SECRET, SO THAT I WOULDN'T GET BEATEN TO THE PUNCH.
NOW THAT EVERYTHING'S READY, IT'S TIME TO ADVISE ROBERT FALCON SCOTT AND HIS TERRA NOVA THAT WE'VE LEFT!
Inform You
MAKE SURE THAT TELEGRAM GETS SENT BEFORE WE SET SAIL.
Beg Inform You Fram Proceeding Antarctic. Amundsen
THE GAUNTLET'S BEEN THROWN DOWN.
THE RACE TO THE SOUTH POLE HAS BEGUN!

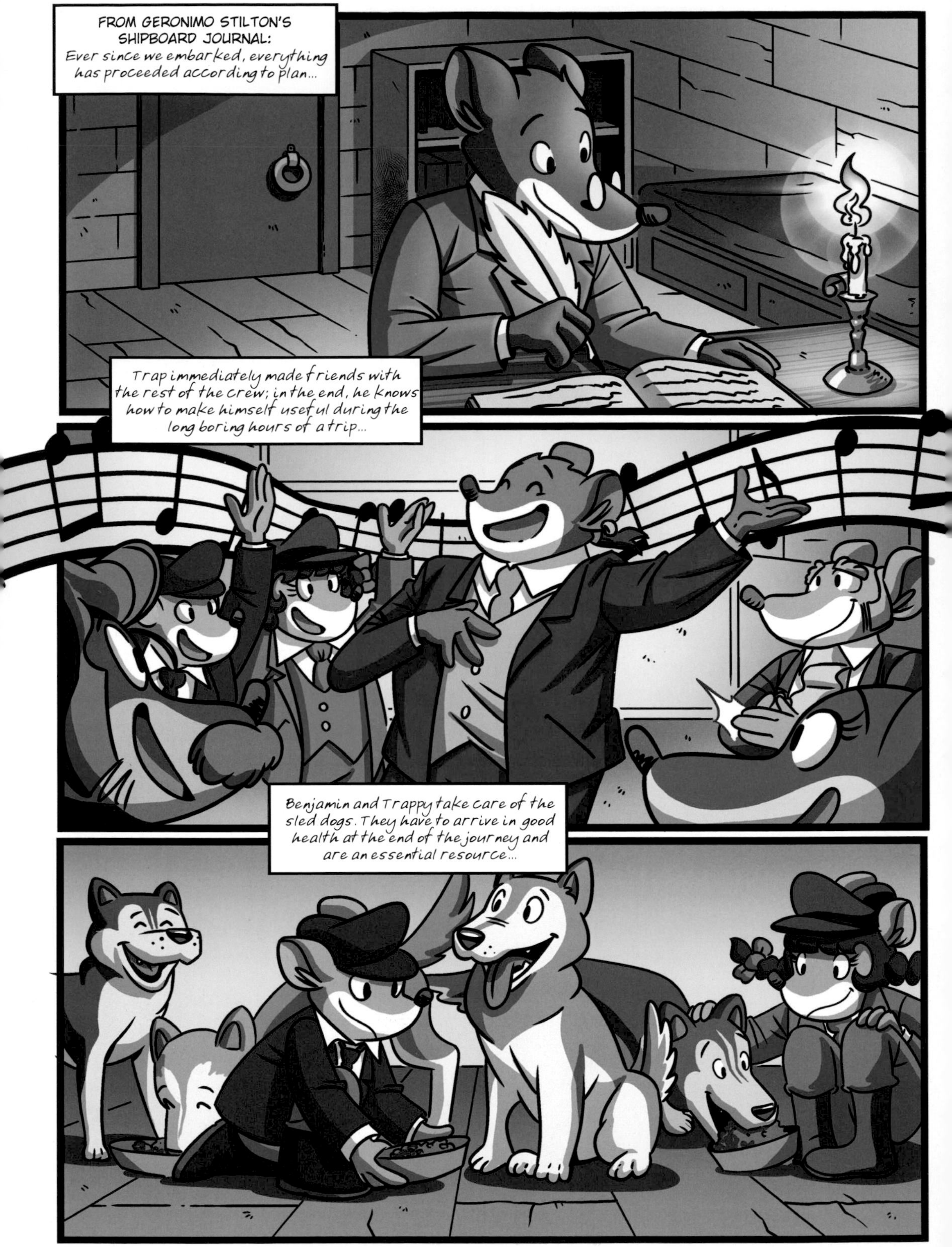
FROM GERONIMO STILTON'S SHIPBOARD JOURNAL:
Ever since we embarked, everything has proceeded according to plan...
Trap immediately made friends with the rest of the crew; in the end, he knows how to make himself useful during the long boring hours of a trip...
Benjamin and Trappy take care of the sled dogs. They have to arrive in good health at the end of the journey and are an essential resource...

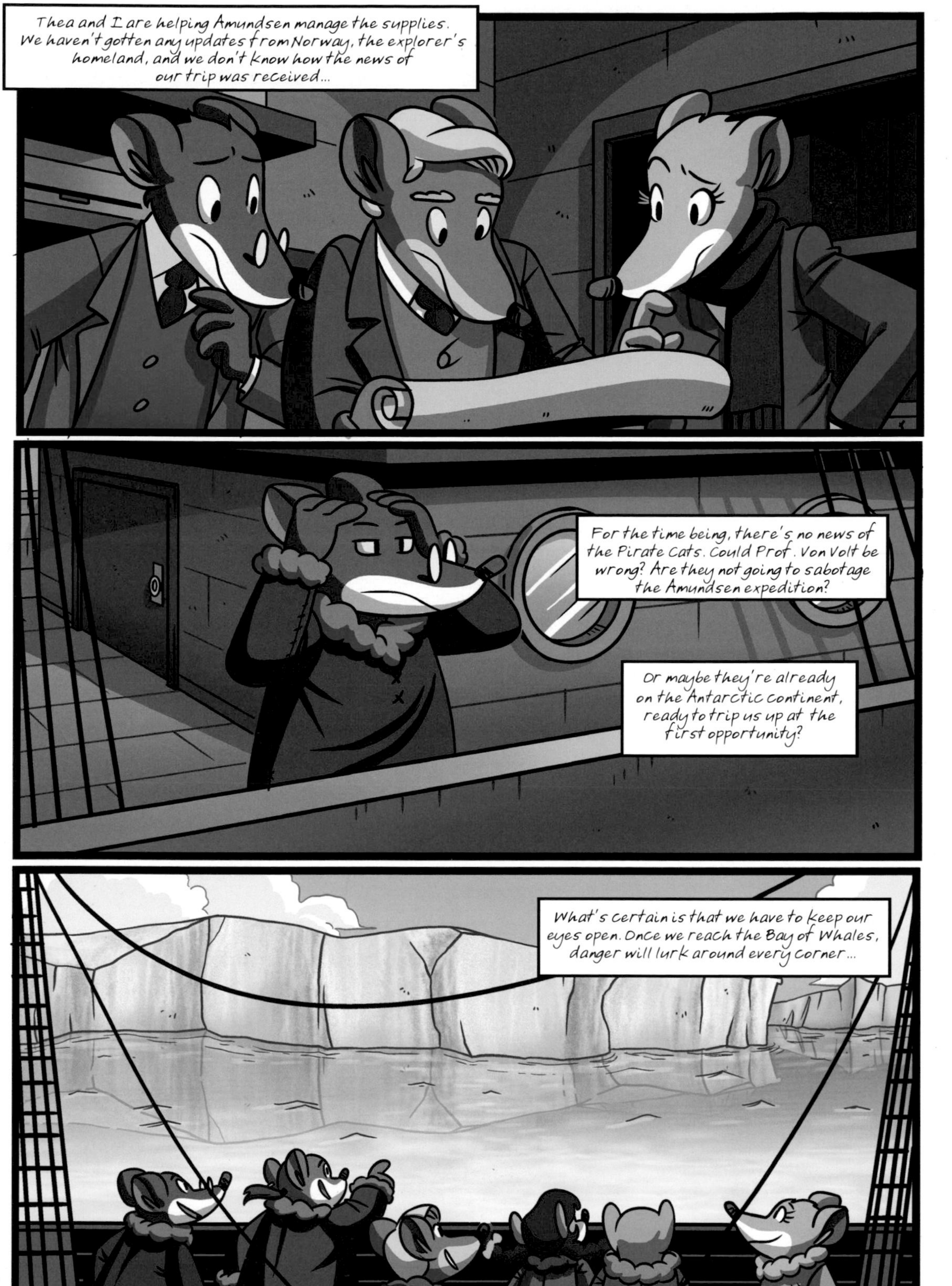
Thea and I are helping Amundsen manage the supplies. We haven't gotten any updates from Norway, the explorer's homeland, and we don't know how the news of our trip was received...
For the time being, there's no news of the Pirate Cats. Could Prof. Von Volt be wrong? Are they not going to sabotage the Amundsen expedition?
Or maybe they're already on the Antarctic continent, ready to trip us up at the first opportunity?
What's certain is that we have to keep our eyes open. Once we reach the Bay of Whales, danger will lurk around every corner...

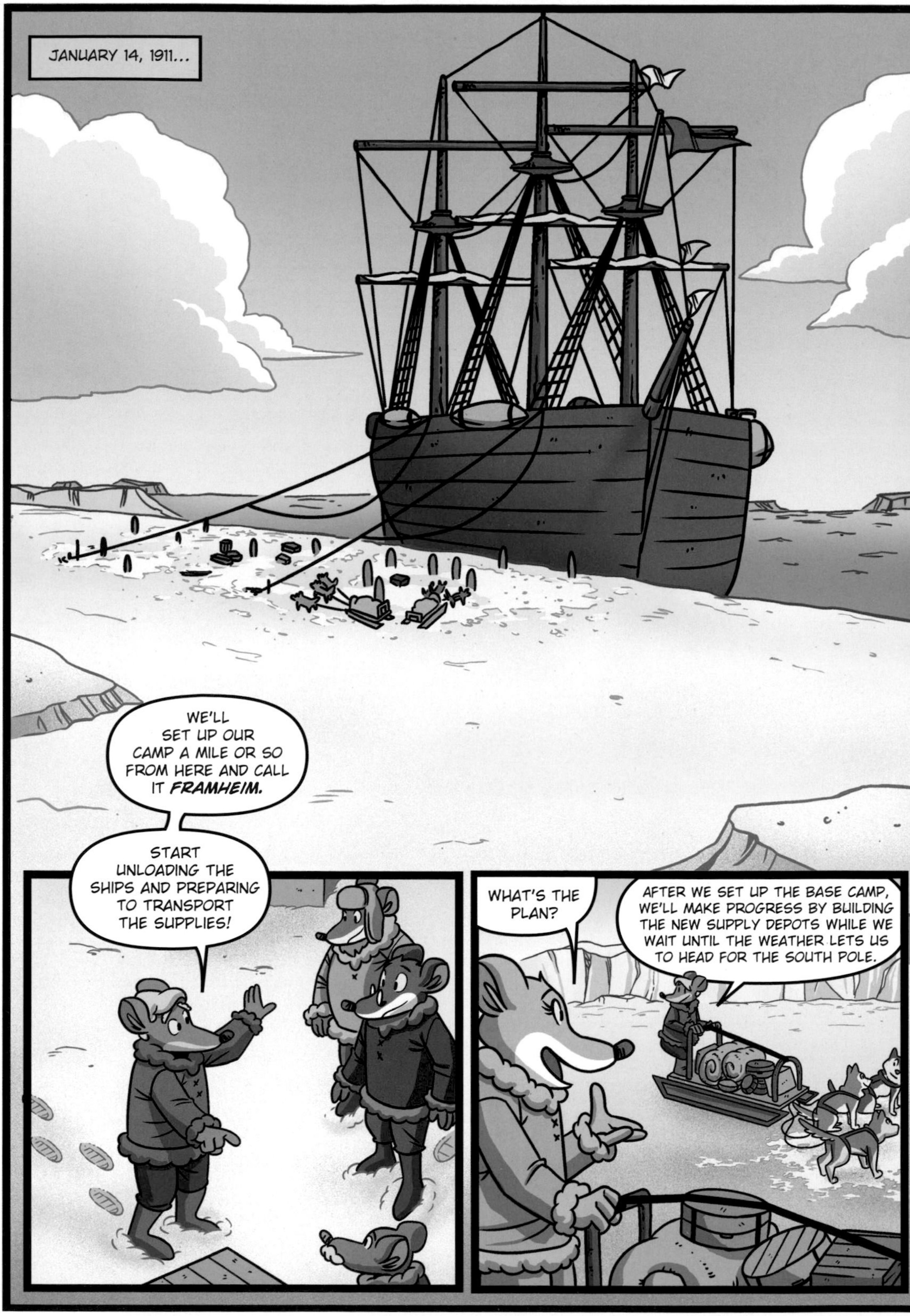
JANUARY 14, 1911...
WE'LL SET UP OUR CAMP A MILE OR SO FROM HERE AND CALL IT FRAMHEIM.
START UNLOADING THE SHIPS AND PREPARING TO TRANSPORT THE SUPPLIES!
WHAT'S THE PLAN?
AFTER WE SET UP THE BASE CAMP, WE'LL MAKE PROGRESS BY BUILDING THE NEW SUPPLY DEPOTS WHILE WE WAIT UNTIL THE WEATHER LETS US TO HEAD FOR THE SOUTH POLE.

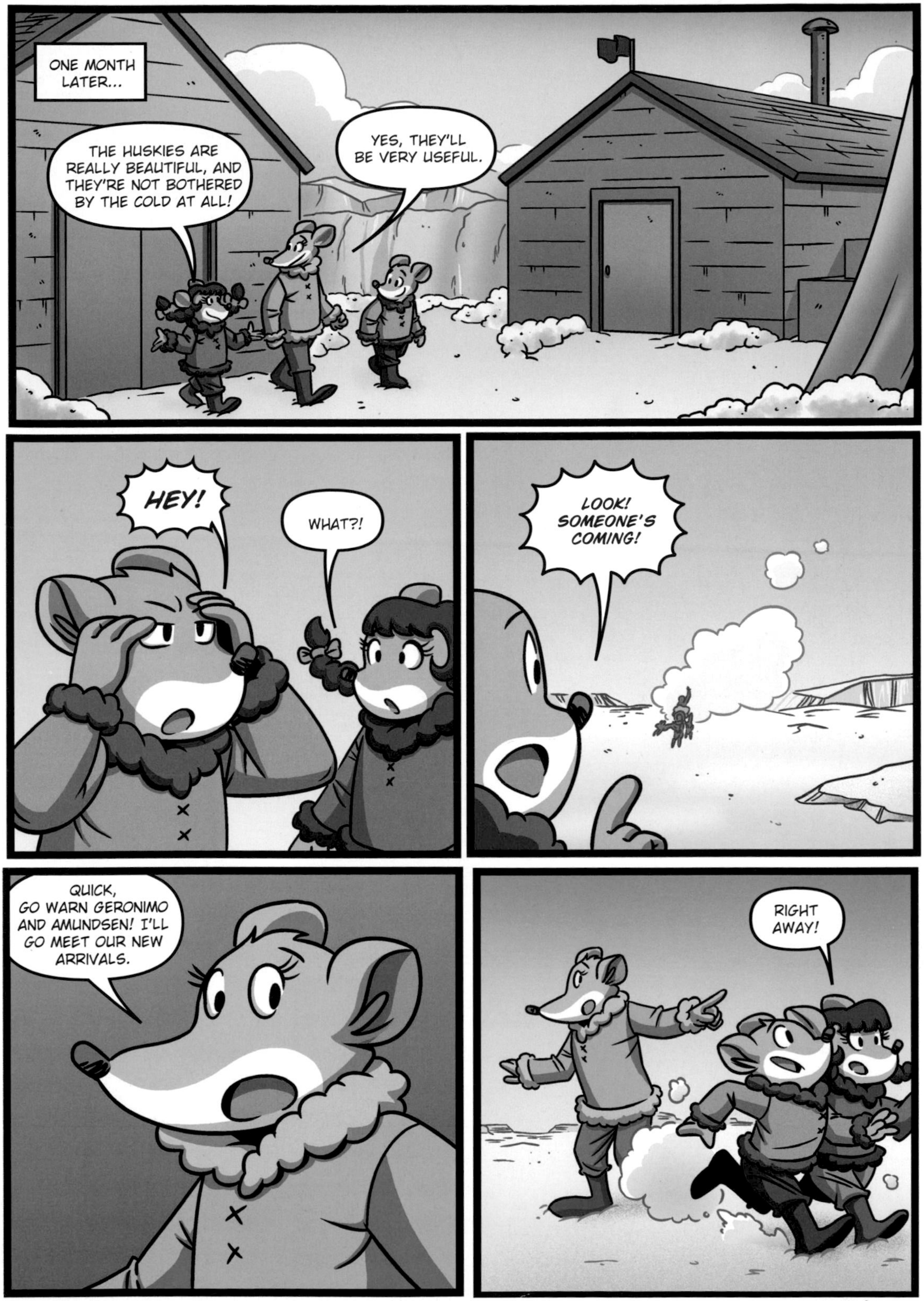
ONE MONTH LATER...
THE HUSKIES ARE REALLY BEAUTIFUL, AND THEY'RE NOT BOTHERED BY THE COLD AT ALL!
YES, THEY'LL BE VERY USEFUL.
HEY!
WHAT?!
LOOK! SOMEONE'S COMING!
QUICK, GO WARN GERONIMO AND AMUNDSEN! I'LL GO MEET OUR NEW ARRIVALS.
RIGHT AWAY!

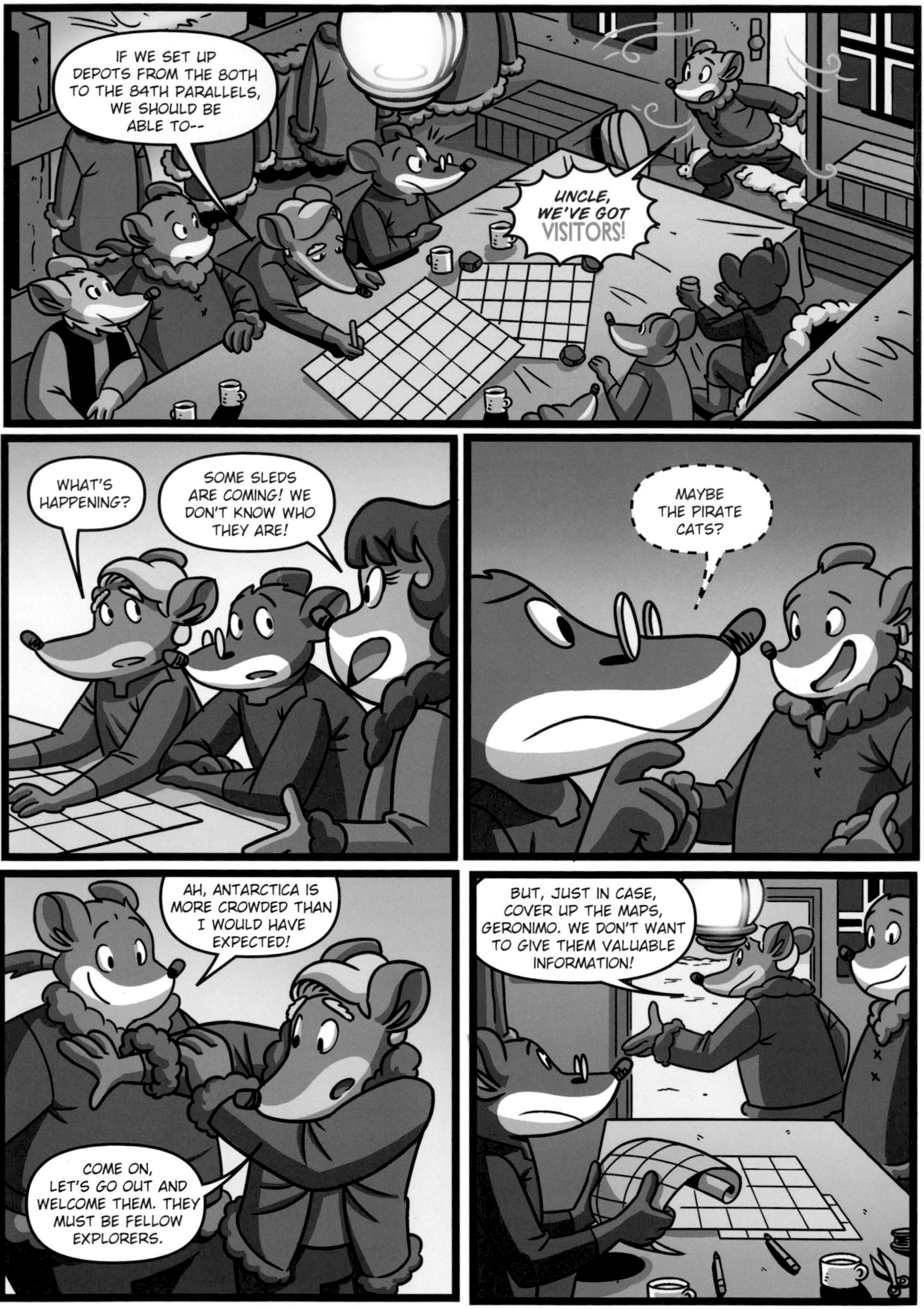

IF WE SET UP DEPOTS FROM THE 80TH TO THE 84TH PARALLELS, WE SHOULD BE ABLE TO--
UNCLE, WE'VE GOT VISITORS!
WHAT'S HAPPENING?
SOME SLEDS ARE COMING! WE DON'T KNOW WHO THEY ARE!
MAYBE THE PIRATE CATS?
AH, ANTARCTICA IS MORE CROWDED THAN I WOULD HAVE EXPECTED!
COME ON, LET'S GO OUT AND WELCOME THEM. THEY MUST BE FELLOW EXPLORERS.
BUT, JUST IN CASE, COVER UP THE MAPS, GERONIMO. WE DON'T WANT TO GIVE THEM VALUABLE INFORMATION!

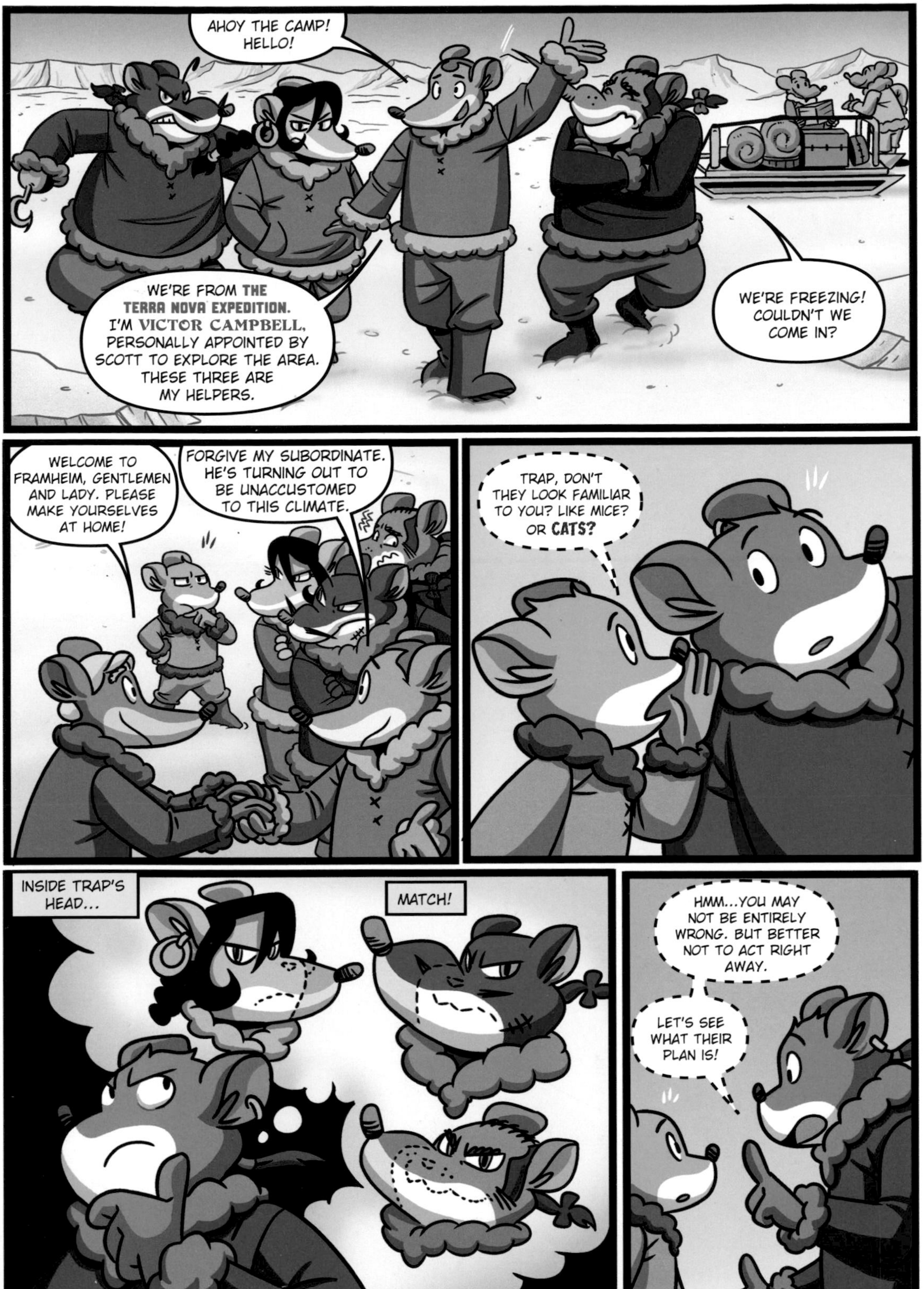
AHOY THE CAMP! HELLO!
WE'RE FROM THE TERRA NOVA EXPEDITION. I'M VICTOR CAMPBELL, PERSONALLY APPOINTED BY SCOTT TO EXPLORE THE AREA. THESE THREE ARE MY HELPERS.
WE'RE FREEZING! COULDN'T WE COME IN?
WELCOME TO FRAMHEIM, GENTLEMEN AND LADY. PLEASE MAKE YOURSELVES AT HOME!
FORGIVE MY SUBORDINATE. HE'S TURNING OUT TO BE UNACCUSTOMED TO THIS CLIMATE.
TRAP, DON'T THEY LOOK FAMILIAR TO YOU? LIKE MICE? OR CATS?
INSIDE TRAP'S HEAD...
MATCH!
HMM...YOU MAY NOT BE ENTIRELY WRONG. BUT BETTER NOT TO ACT RIGHT AWAY.
LET'S SEE WHAT THEIR PLAN IS!

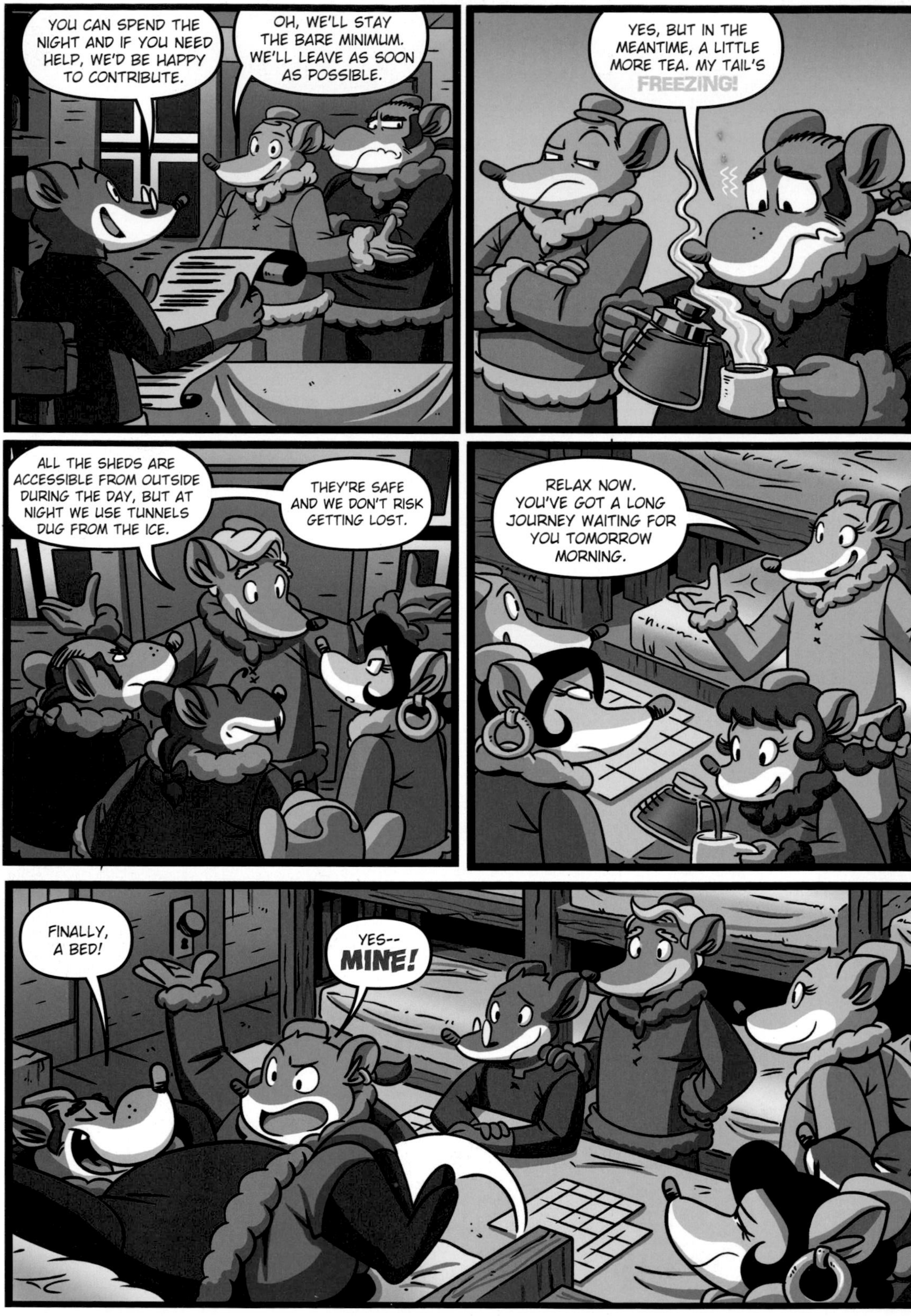
YOU CAN SPEND THE NIGHT AND IF YOU NEED HELP, WE'D BE HAPPY TO CONTRIBUTE.
OH, WE'LL STAY THE BARE MINIMUM. WE'LL LEAVE AS SOON AS POSSIBLE.
YES, BUT IN THE MEANTIME, A LITTLE MORE TEA. MY TAIL'S FREEZING!
ALL THE SHEDS ARE ACCESSIBLE FROM OUTSIDE DURING THE DAY, BUT AT NIGHT WE USE TUNNELS DUG FROM THE ICE.
THEY'RE SAFE AND WE DON'T RISK GETTING LOST.
RELAX NOW. YOU'VE GOT A LONG JOURNEY WAITING FOR YOU TOMORROW MORNING.
FINALLY, A BED!
YES-- MINE!

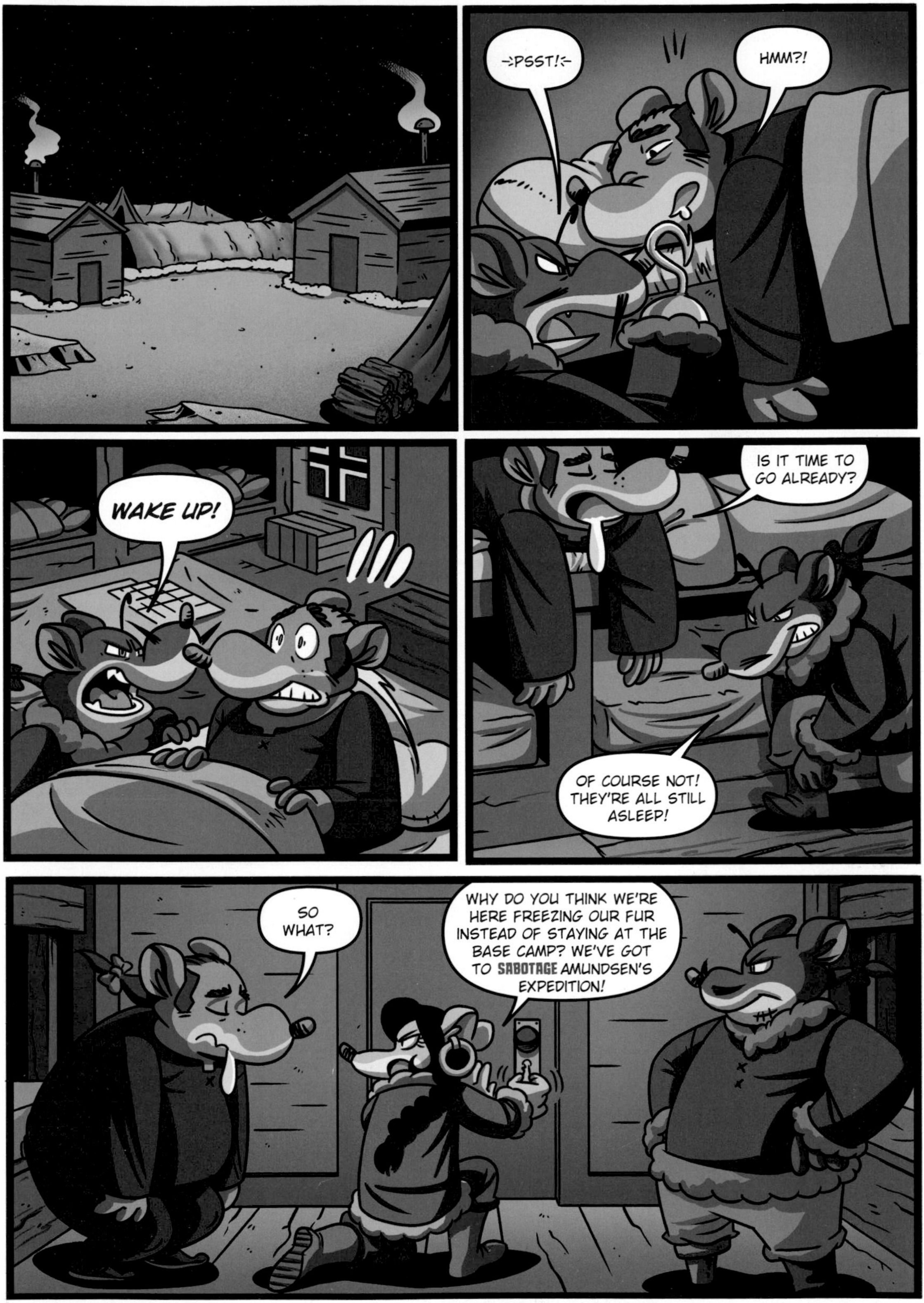
-PSST!-
HMM?!
WAKE UP!
IS IT TIME TO GO ALREADY?
OF COURSE NOT! THEY'RE ALL STILL ASLEEP!
SO WHAT?
WHY DO YOU THINK WE'RE HERE FREEZING OUR FUR INSTEAD OF STAYING AT THE BASE CAMP? WE'VE GOT TO SABOTAGE AMUNDSEN'S EXPEDITION!

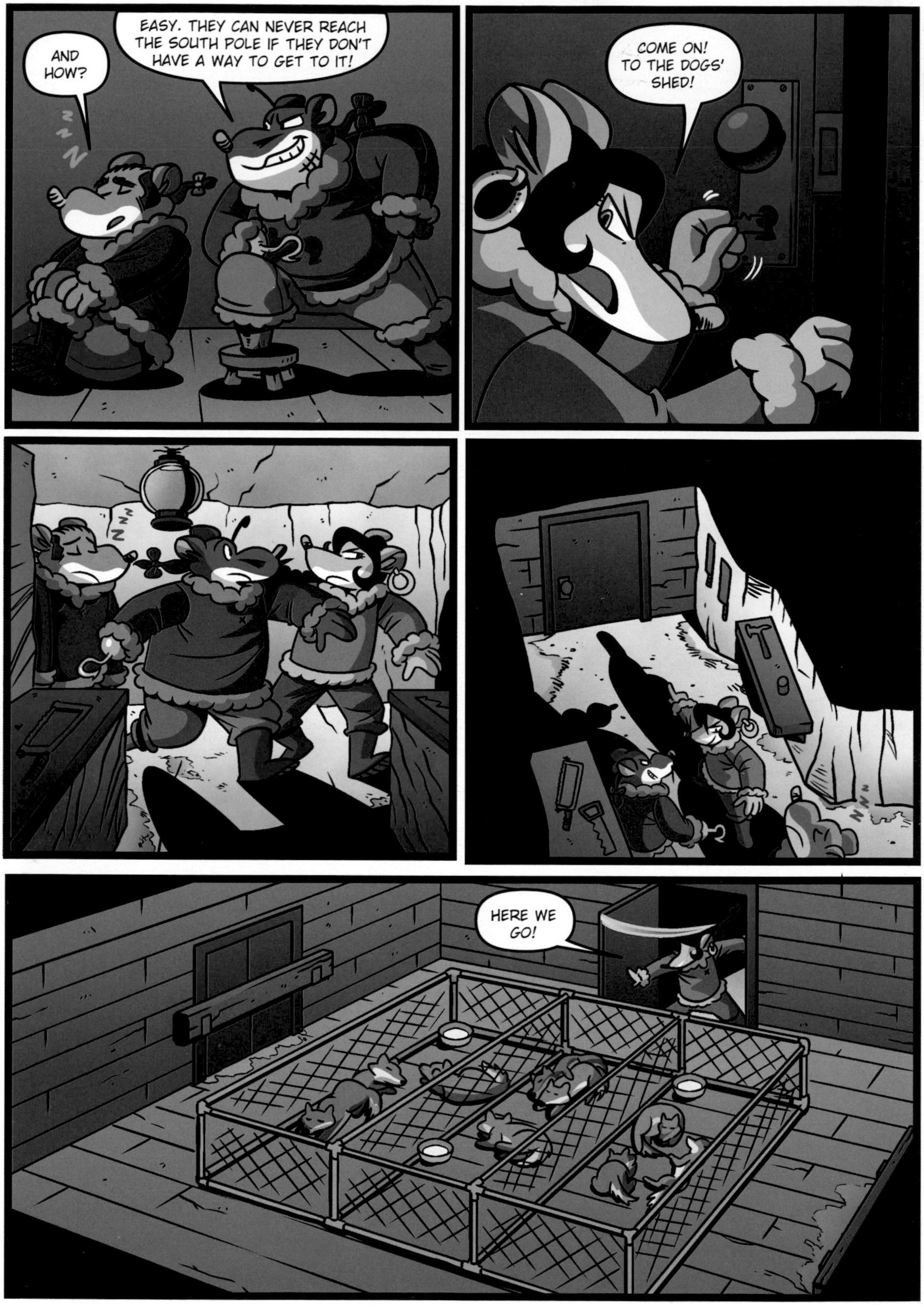
AND HOW?
EASY. THEY CAN NEVER REACH THE SOUTH POLE IF THEY DON'T HAVE A WAY TO GET TO IT!
COME ON! TO THE DOGS' SHED!
HERE WE GO!

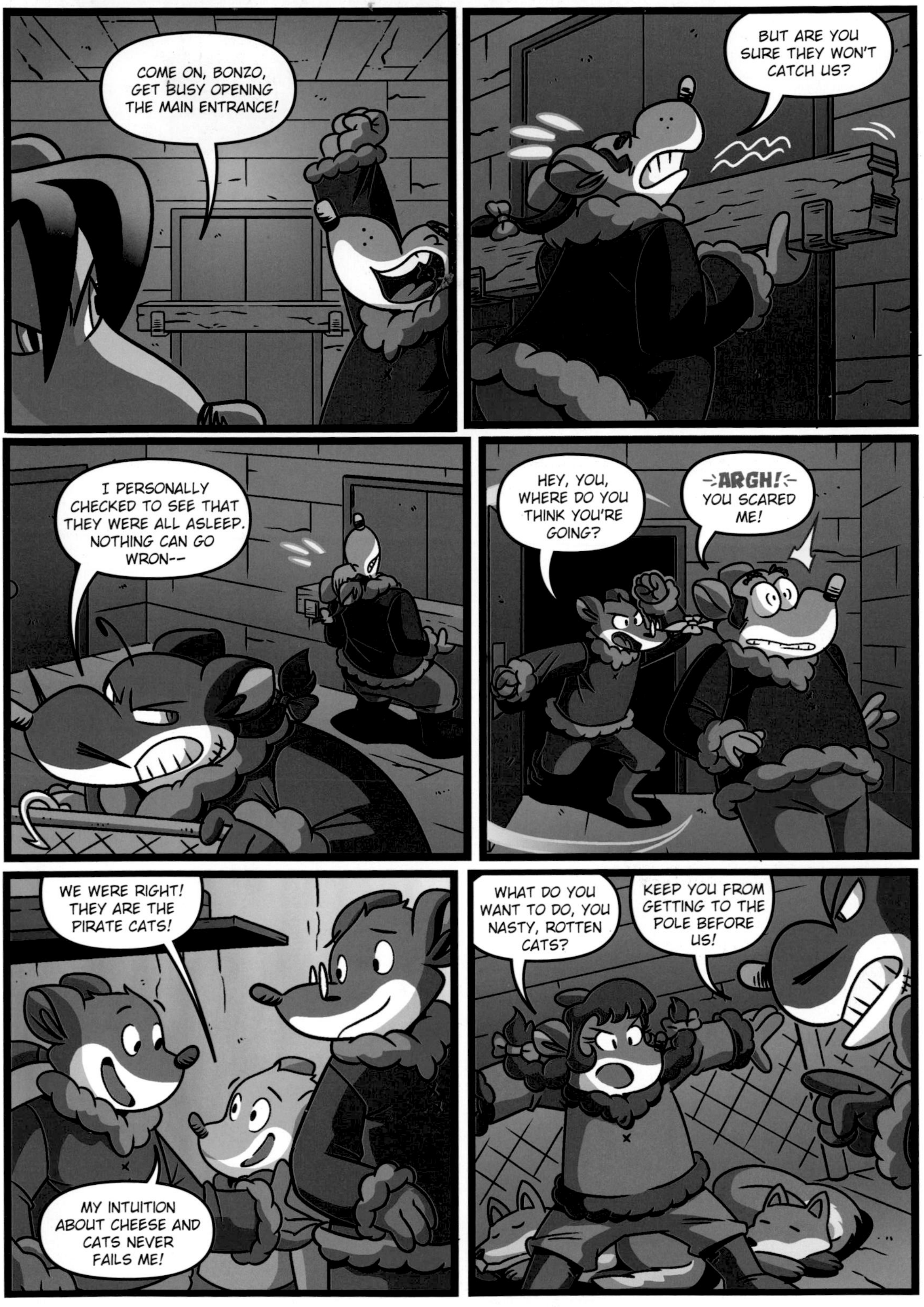
COME ON, BONZO, GET BUSY OPENING THE MAIN ENTRANCE!
BUT ARE YOU SURE THEY WON'T CATCH US?
I PERSONALLY CHECKED TO SEE THAT THEY WERE ALL ASLEEP. NOTHING CAN GO WRON--
HEY, YOU, WHERE DO YOU THINK YOU'RE GOING?
ARGH! YOU SCARED ME!
WE WERE RIGHT! THEY ARE THE PIRATE CATS!
MY INTUITION ABOUT CHEESE AND CATS NEVER FAILS ME!
WHAT DO YOU WANT TO DO, YOU NASTY, ROTTEN CATS?
KEEP YOU FROM GETTING TO THE POLE BEFORE US!

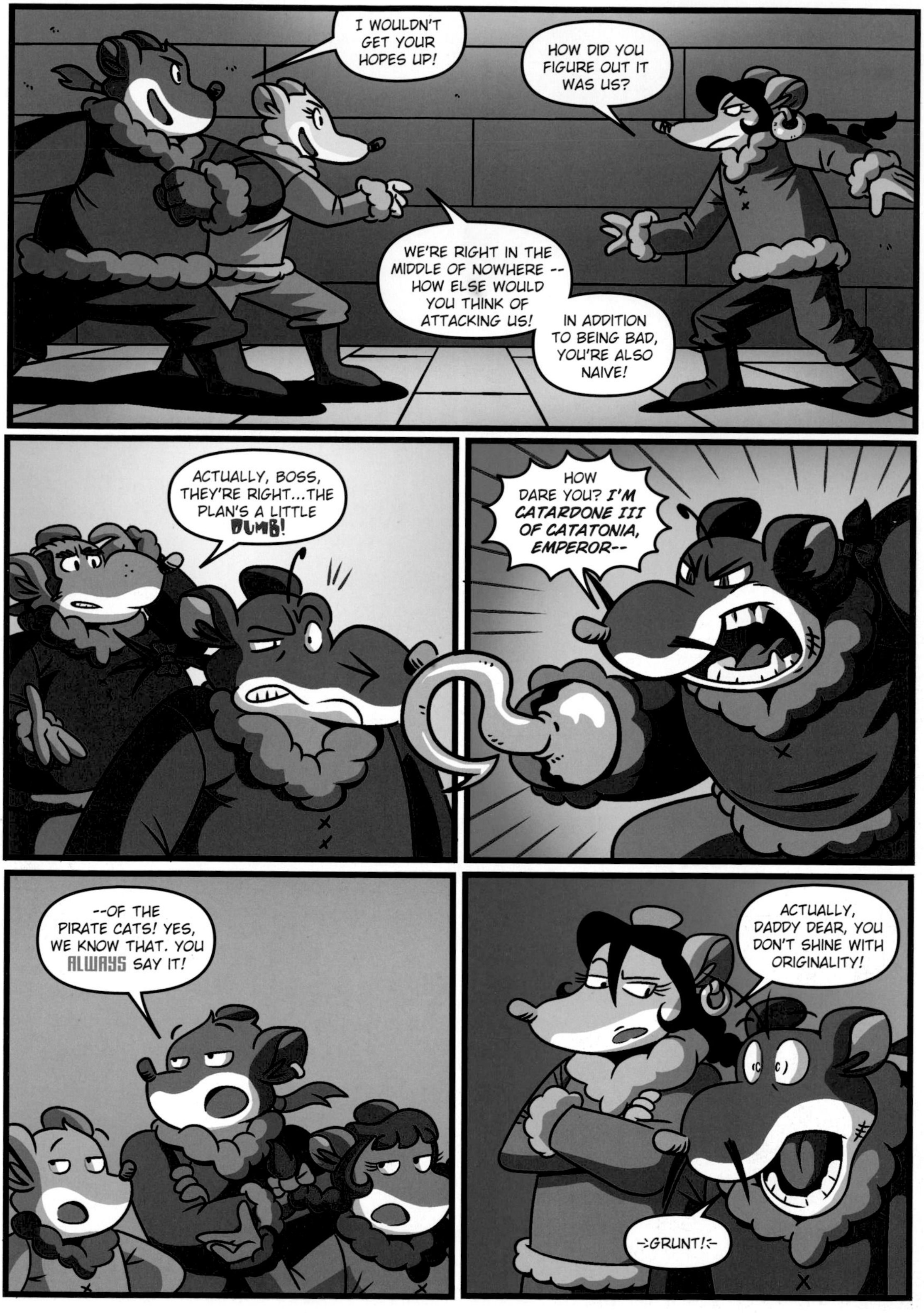
I WOULDN'T GET YOUR HOPES UP!
HOW DID YOU FIGURE OUT IT WAS US?
WE'RE RIGHT IN THE MIDDLE OF NOWHERE -- HOW ELSE WOULD YOU THINK OF ATTACKING US!
IN ADDITION TO BEING BAD, YOU'RE ALSO NAIVE!
ACTUALLY, BOSS, THEY'RE RIGHT...THE PLAN'S A LITTLE DUMB!
HOW DARE YOU? I'M CATARDONE III OF CATATONIA, EMPEROR--
--OF THE PIRATE CATS! YES, WE KNOW THAT. YOU ALWAYS SAY IT!
ACTUALLY, DADDY DEAR, YOU DON'T SHINE WITH ORIGINALITY!
GRUNT!

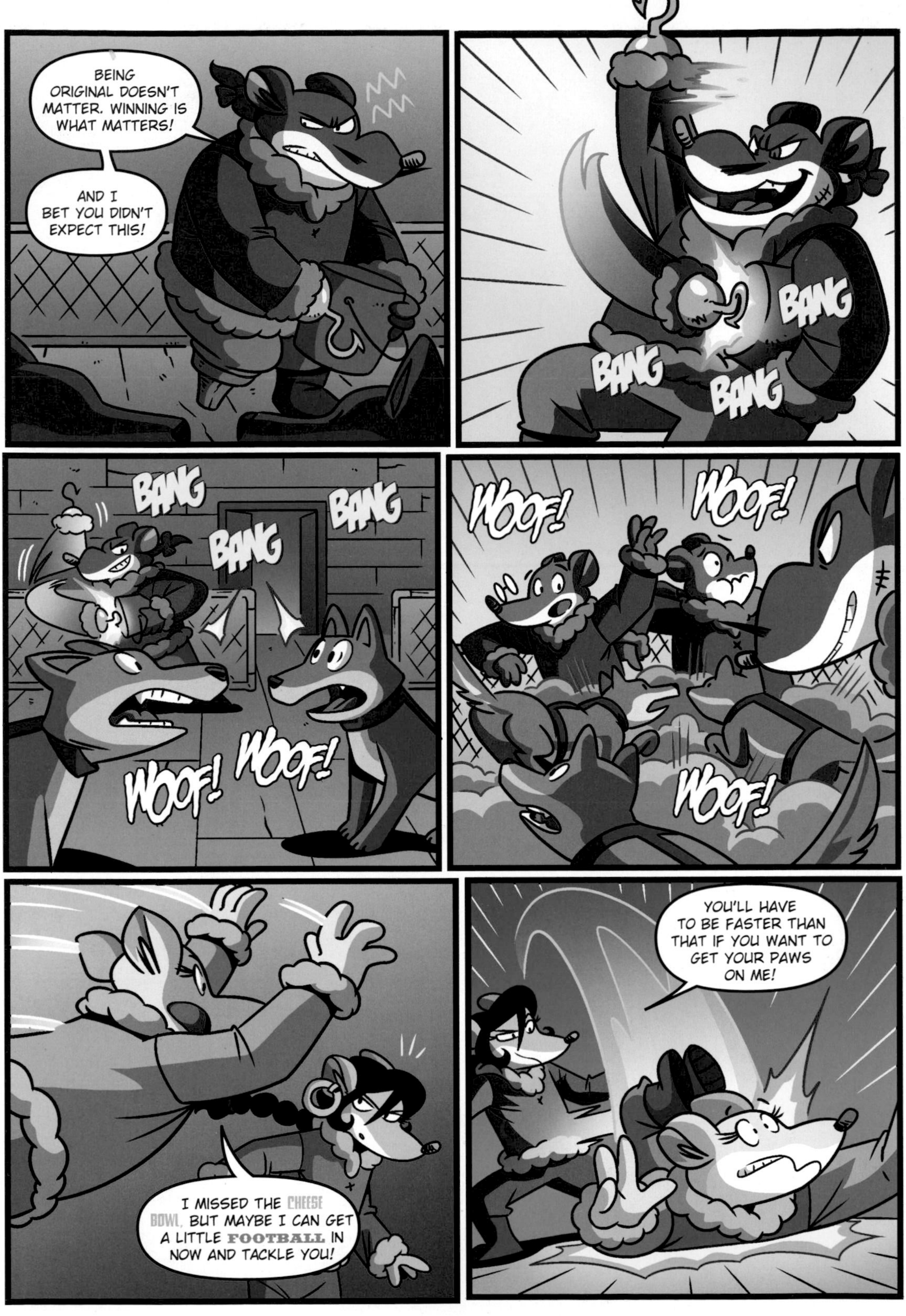

BEING ORIGINAL DOESN'T MATTER. WINNING IS WHAT MATTERS!
AND I BET YOU DIDN'T EXPECT THIS!
BANG
BANG
BANG
BANG
BANG
BANG
WOOF!
WOOF!
WOOF!
WOOF!
WOOF!
I MISSED THE CHEESE BOWL, BUT MAYBE I CAN GET A LITTLE FOOTBALL IN NOW AND TACKLE YOU!
YOU'LL HAVE TO BE FASTER THAN THAT IF YOU WANT TO GET YOUR PAWS ON ME!

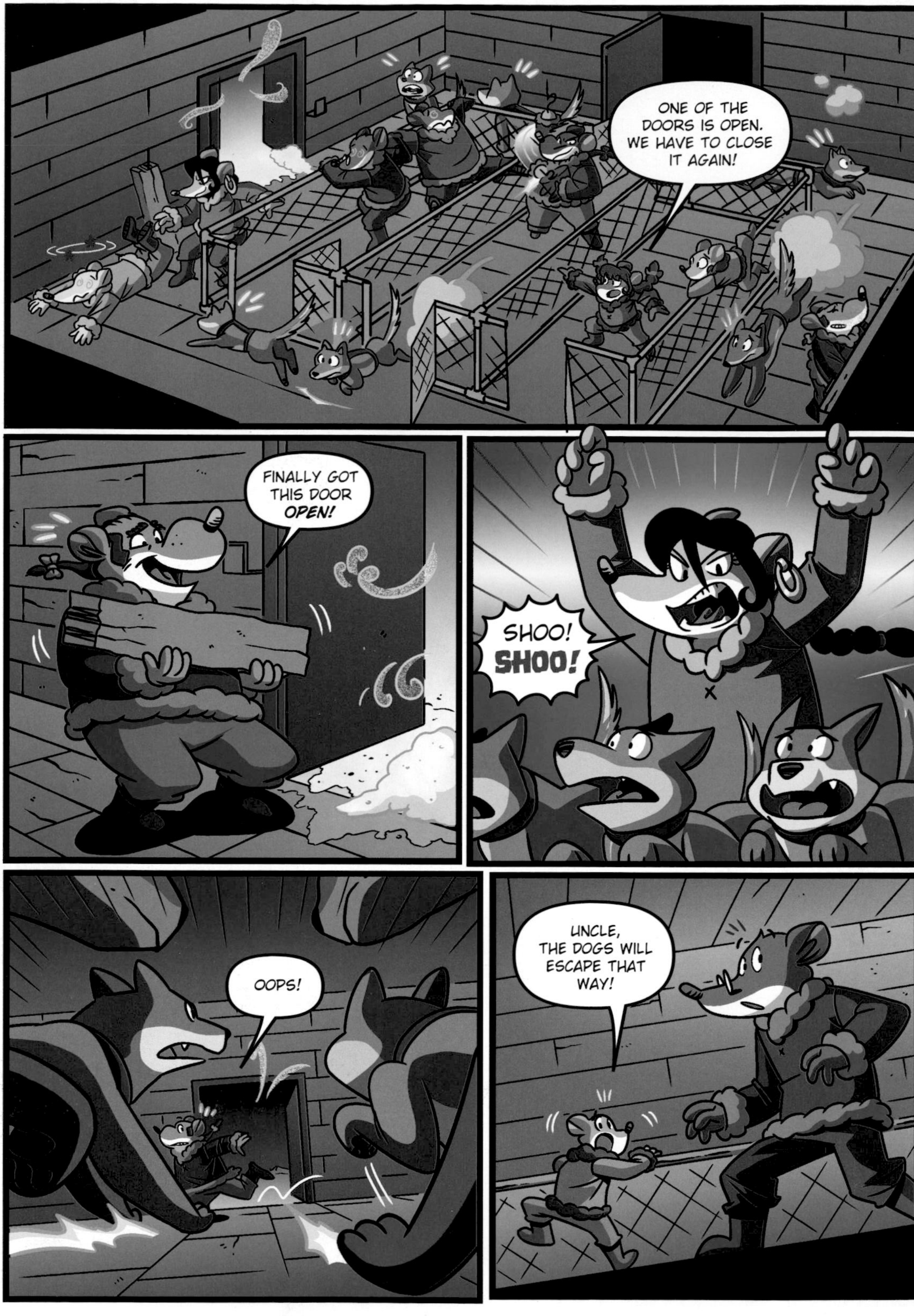
ONE OF THE DOORS IS OPEN. WE HAVE TO CLOSE IT AGAIN!
FINALLY GOT THIS DOOR OPEN!
SHOO! SHOO!
OOPS!
UNCLE, THE DOGS WILL ESCAPE THAT WAY!

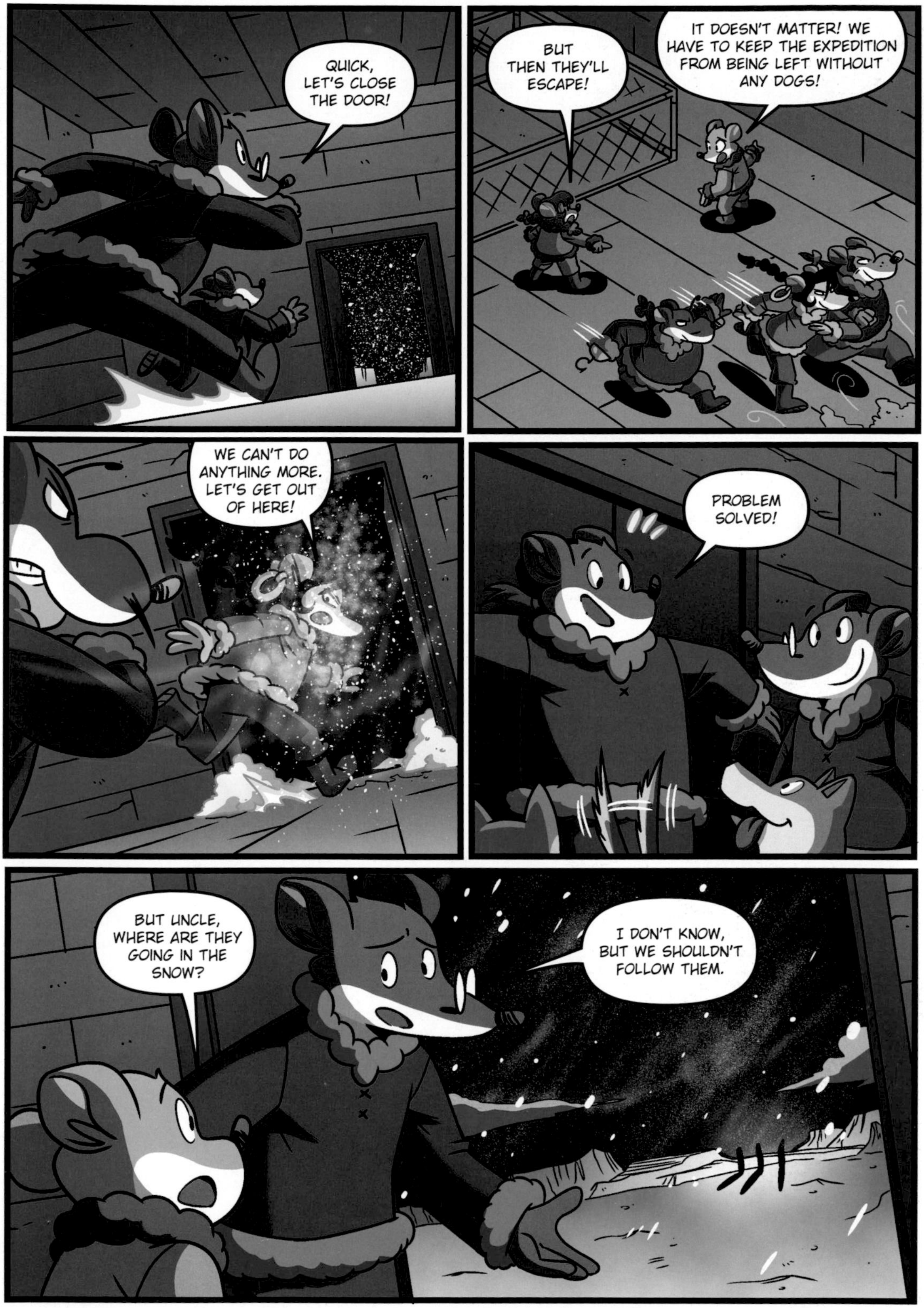
QUICK, LET'S CLOSE THE DOOR!
BUT THEN THEY'LL ESCAPE!
IT DOESN'T MATTER! WE HAVE TO KEEP THE EXPEDITION FROM BEING LEFT WITHOUT ANY DOGS!
WE CAN'T DO ANYTHING MORE. LET'S GET OUT OF HERE!
PROBLEM SOLVED!
BUT UNCLE, WHERE ARE THEY GOING IN THE SNOW?
I DON'T KNOW, BUT WE SHOULDN'T FOLLOW THEM.

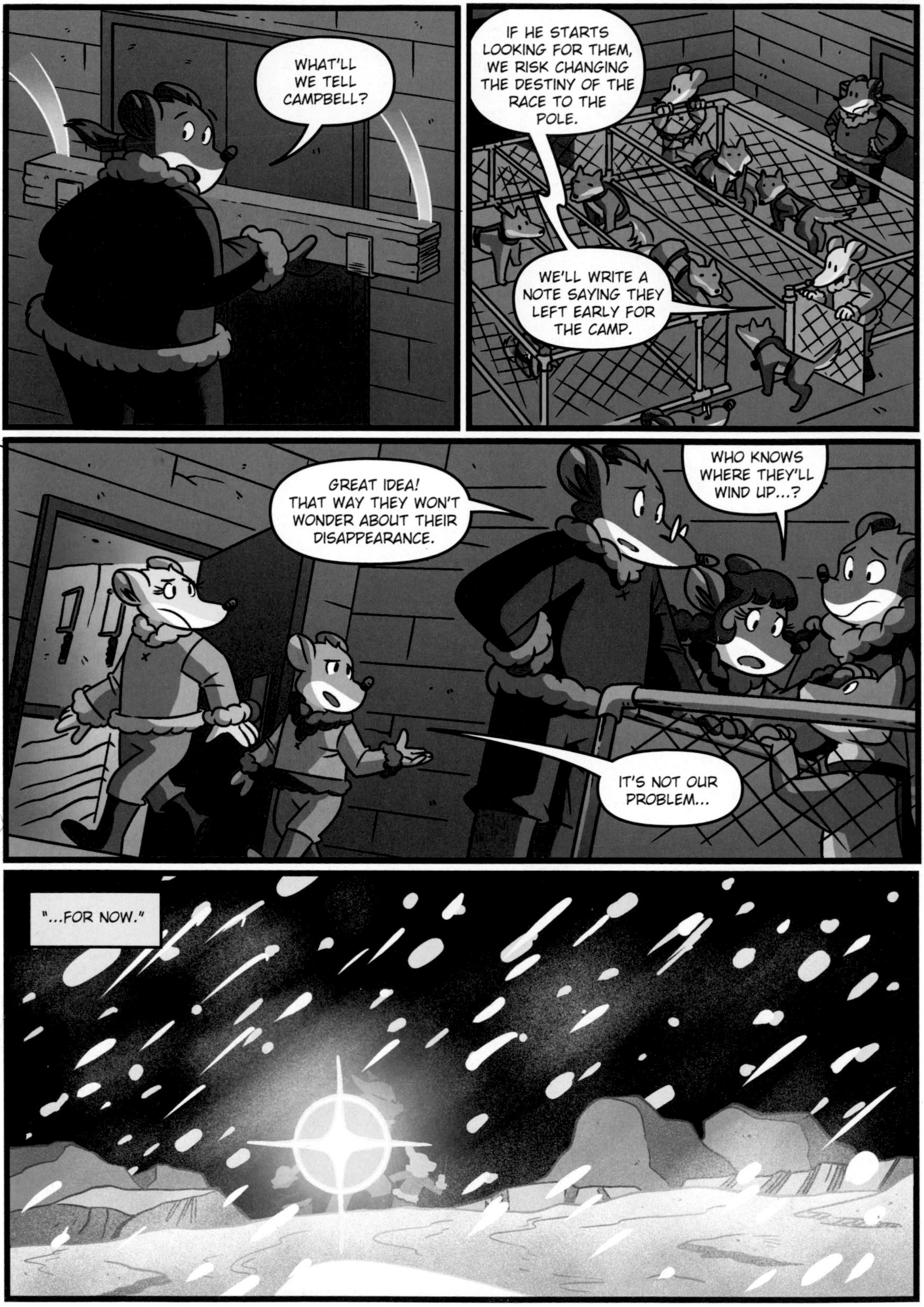
WHAT'LL WE TELL CAMPBELL?
IF HE STARTS LOOKING FOR THEM, WE RISK CHANGING THE DESTINY OF THE RACE TO THE POLE.
WE'LL WRITE A NOTE SAYING THEY LEFT EARLY FOR THE CAMP.
GREAT IDEA! THAT WAY THEY WON'T WONDER ABOUT THEIR DISAPPEARANCE.
WHO KNOWS WHERE THEY'LL WIND UP...?
IT'S NOT OUR PROBLEM...
"...FOR NOW."

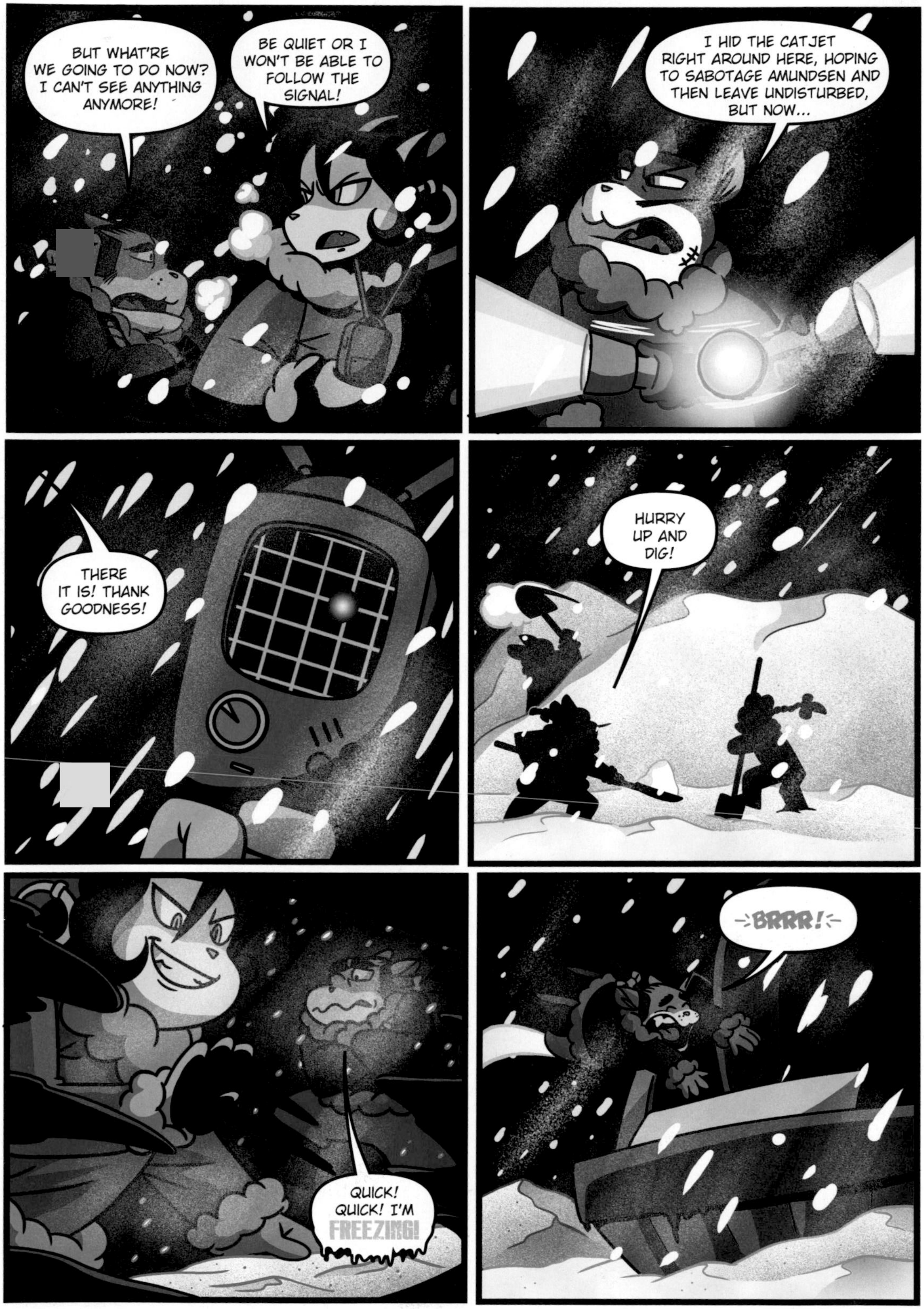
BUT WHAT'RE WE GOING TO DO NOW? I CAN'T SEE ANYTHING ANYMORE!
BE QUIET OR I WON'T BE ABLE TO FOLLOW THE SIGNAL!
I HID THE CATJET RIGHT AROUND HERE, HOPING TO SABOTAGE AMUNDSEN AND THEN LEAVE UNDISTURBED, BUT NOW...
THERE IT IS! THANK GOODNESS!
HURRY UP AND DIG!
QUICK! QUICK! I'M FREEZING!
BRRR!

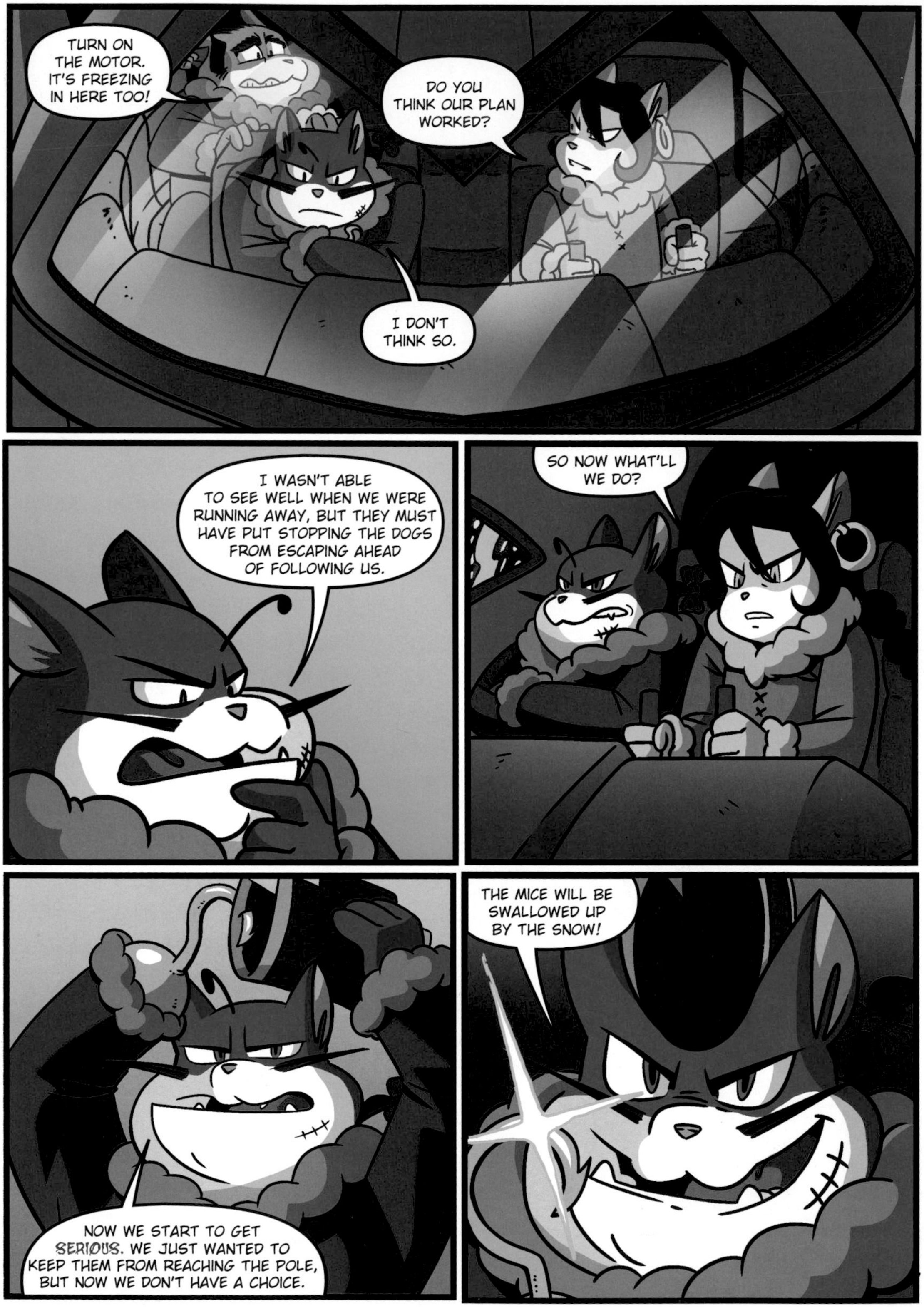
TURN ON THE MOTOR. IT'S FREEZING IN HERE TOO!
DO YOU THINK OUR PLAN WORKED?
I DON'T THINK SO.
I WASN'T ABLE TO SEE WELL WHEN WE WERE RUNNING AWAY, BUT THEY MUST HAVE PUT STOPPING THE DOGS FROM ESCAPING AHEAD OF FOLLOWING US.
SO NOW WHAT'LL WE DO?
NOW WE START TO GET SERIOUS. WE JUST WANTED TO KEEP THEM FROM REACHING THE POLE, BUT NOW WE DON'T HAVE A CHOICE.
THE MICE WILL BE SWALLOWED UP BY THE SNOW!

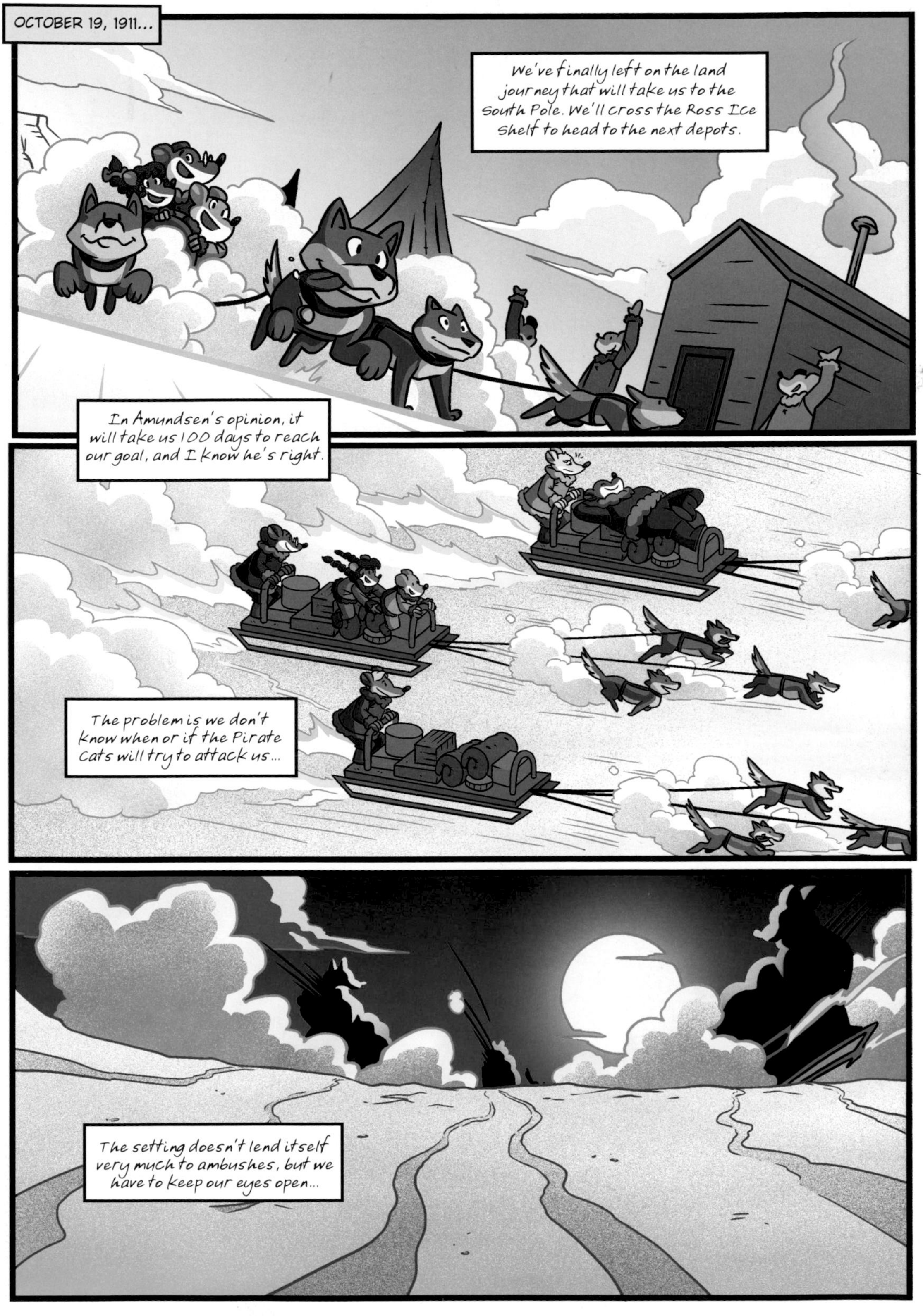
OCTOBER 19, 1911...
We've finally left on the land journey that will take us to the South Pole. We'll cross the Ross Ice Shelf to head to the next depots.
In Amundsen's opinion, it will take us 100 days to reach our goal, and I know he's right.
The problem is we don't know when or if the Pirate Cats will try to attack us...
The setting doesn't lend itself very much to ambushes, but we have to keep our eyes open...

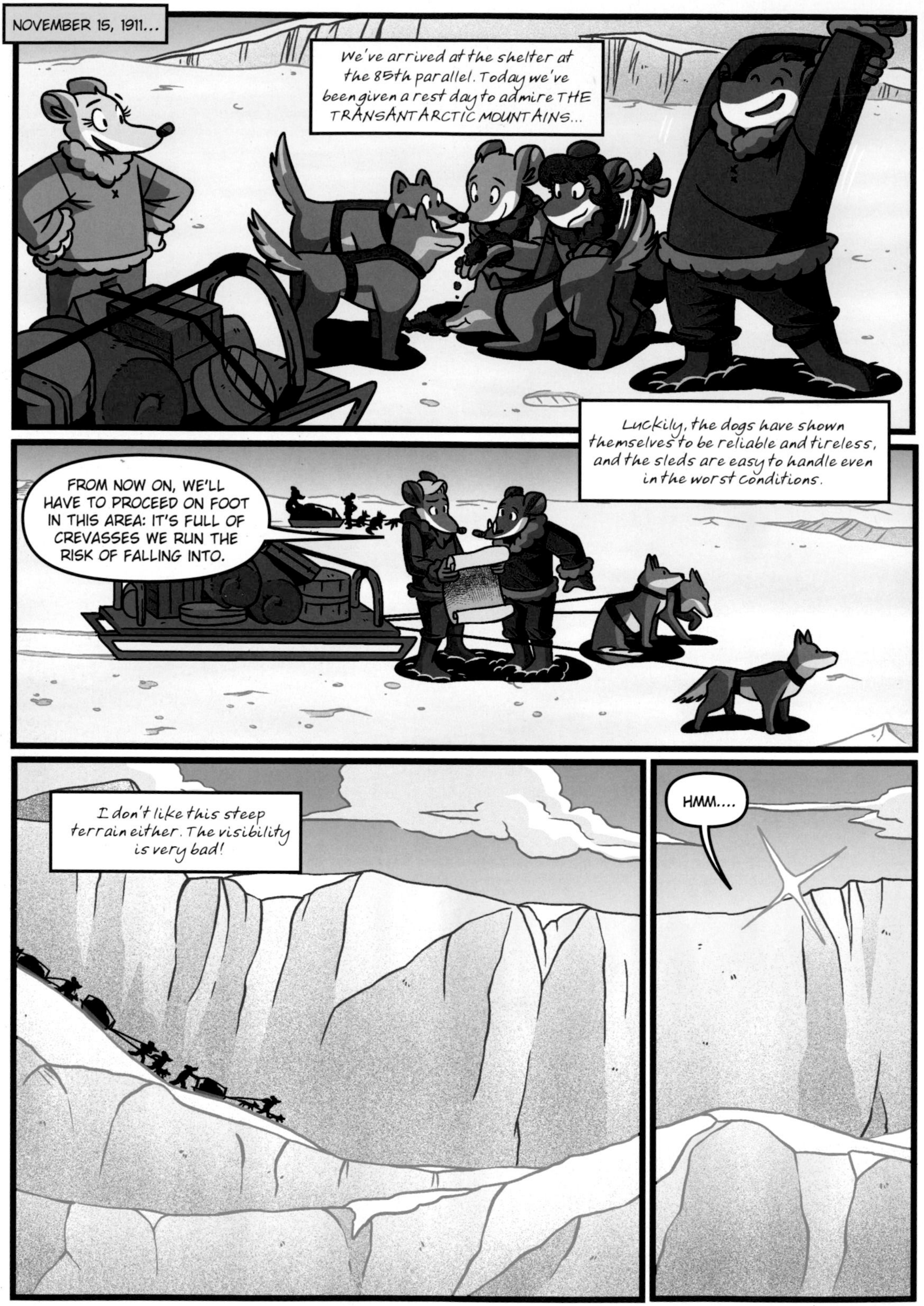
NOVEMBER 15, 1911...
We've arrived at the shelter at the 85th parallel. Today we've been given a rest day to admire THE TRANSANTARCTIC MOUNTAINS...
Luckily, the dogs have shown themselves to be reliable and tireless, and the sleds are easy to handle even in the worst conditions.
FROM NOW ON, WE'LL HAVE TO PROCEED ON FOOT IN THIS AREA: IT'S FULL OF CREVASSES WE RUN THE RISK OF FALLING INTO.
I don't like this steep terrain either. The visibility is very bad!
HMM....

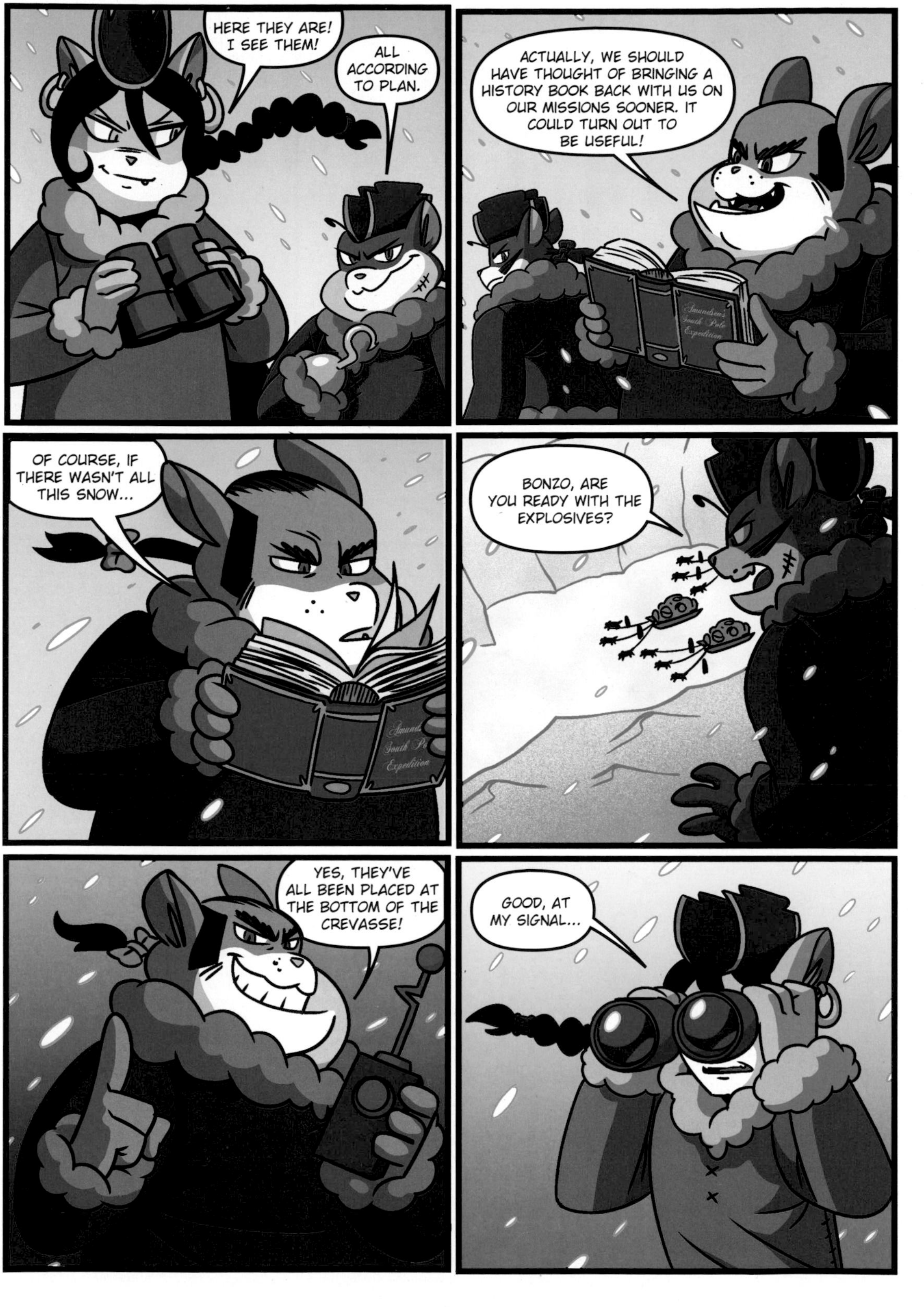
HERE THEY ARE! I SEE THEM!
ALL ACCORDING TO PLAN.
ACTUALLY, WE SHOULD HAVE THOUGHT OF BRINGING A HISTORY BOOK BACK WITH US ON OUR MISSIONS SOONER. IT COULD TURN OUT TO BE USEFUL!
Amundsen's South Pole Expedition
OF COURSE, IF THERE WASN'T ALL THIS SNOW...
BONZO, ARE YOU READY WITH THE EXPLOSIVES?
YES, THEY'VE ALL BEEN PLACED AT THE BOTTOM OF THE CREVASSE!
GOOD, AT MY SIGNAL...

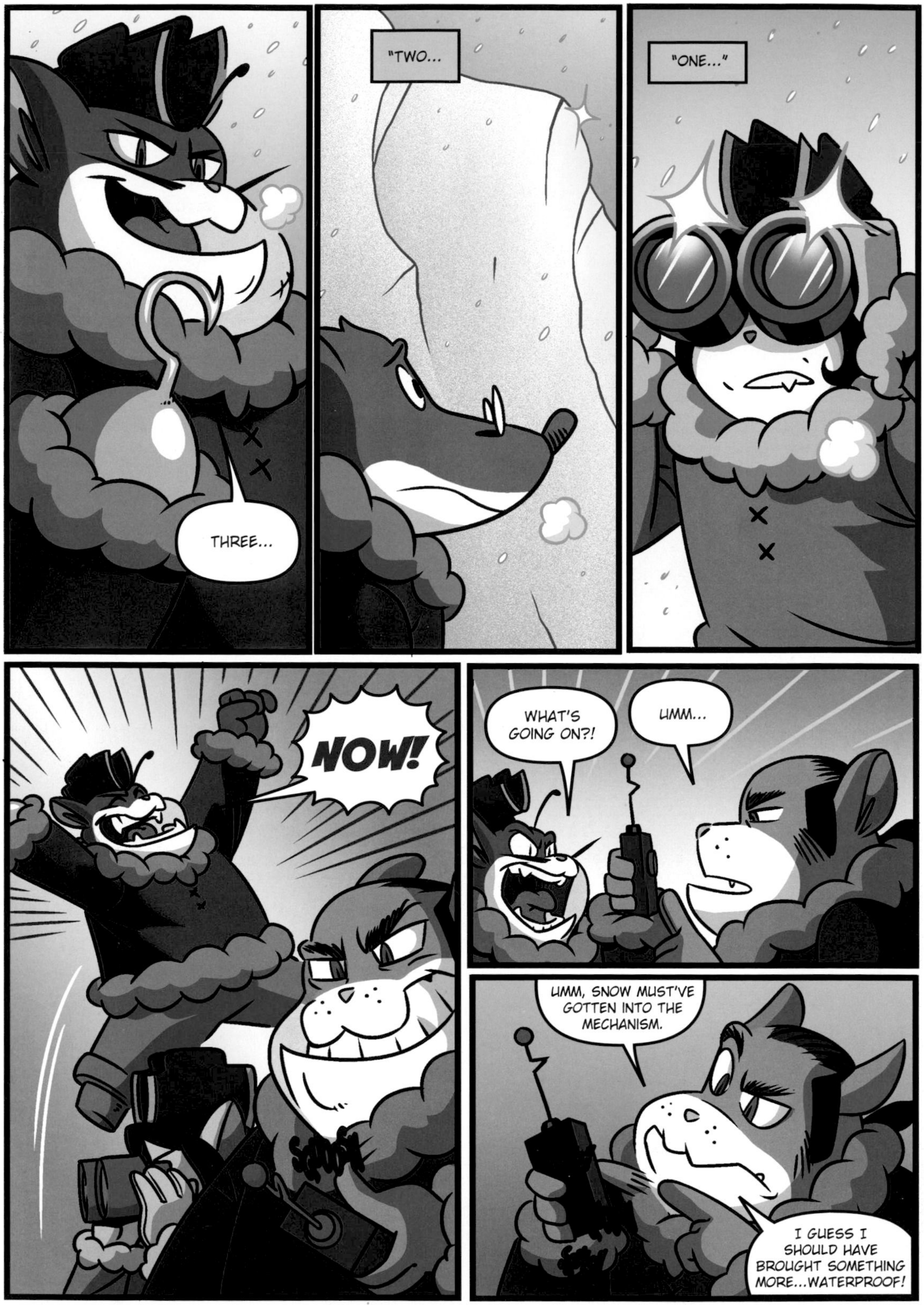
THREE...
"TWO...
"ONE..."
NOW!
WHAT'S GOING ON?!
UMM...
UMM, SNOW MUST'VE GOTTEN INTO THE MECHANISM.
I GUESS I SHOULD HAVE BROUGHT SOMETHING MORE...WATERPROOF!

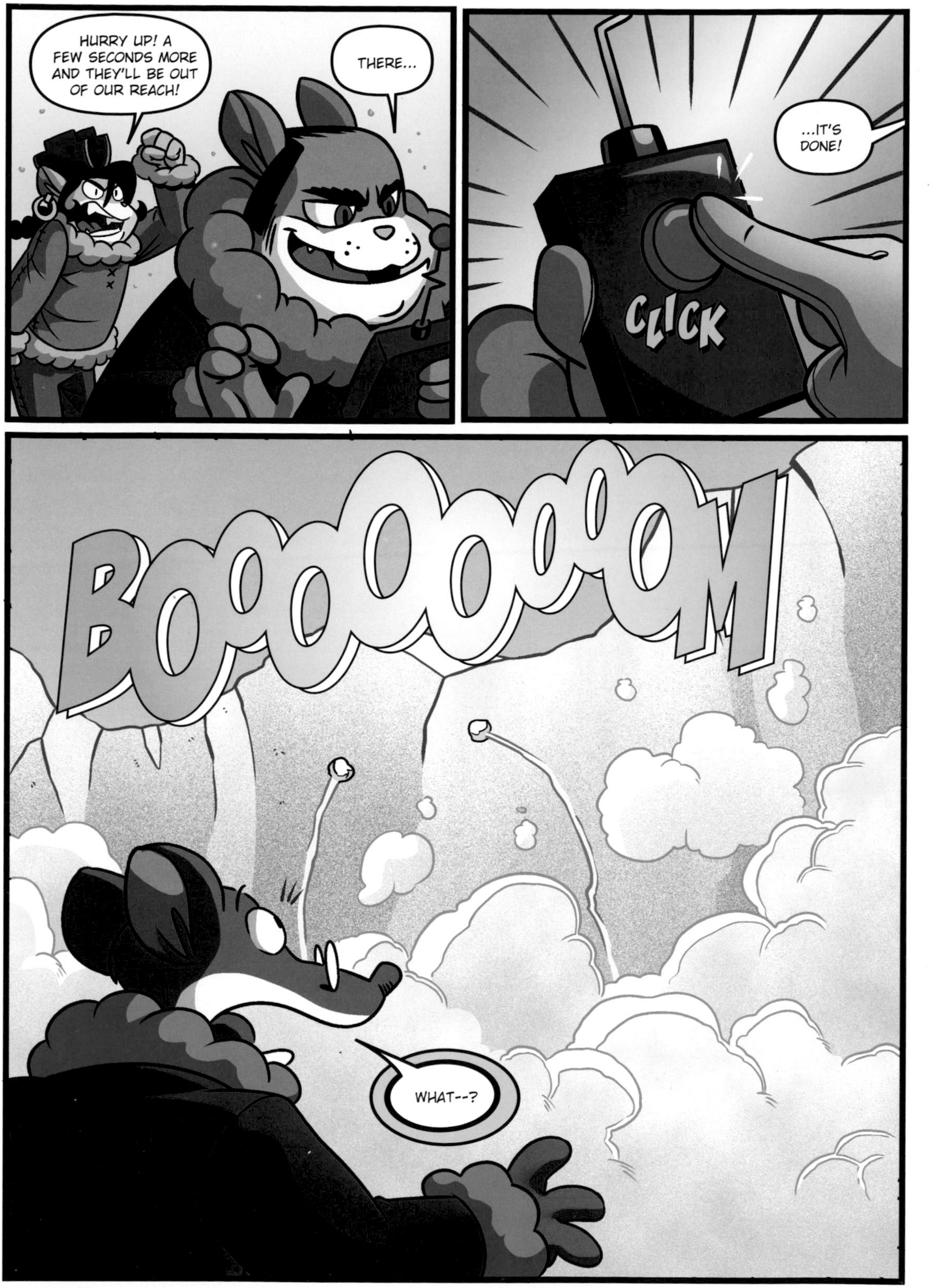
HURRY UP! A FEW SECONDS MORE AND THEY'LL BE OUT OF OUR REACH!
THERE...
...IT'S DONE!
CLICK
BOOOOOOOOM
WHAT--?

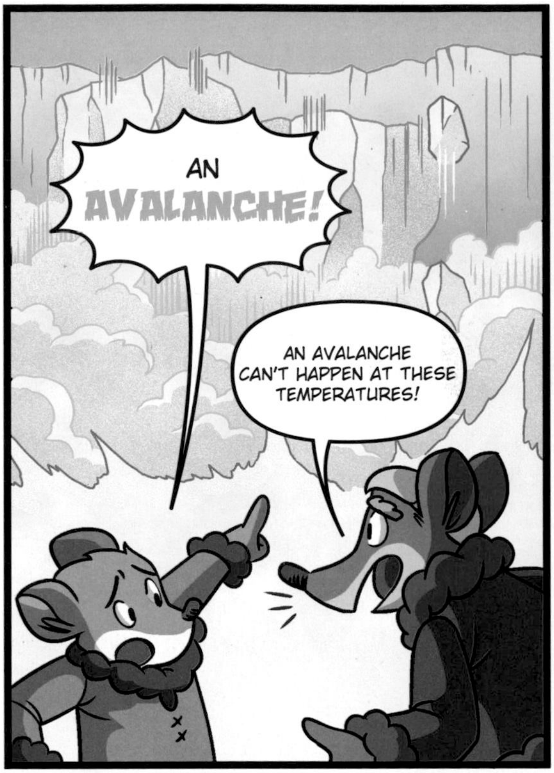
AN AVALANCHE!
AN AVALANCHE CAN'T HAPPEN AT THESE TEMPERATURES!

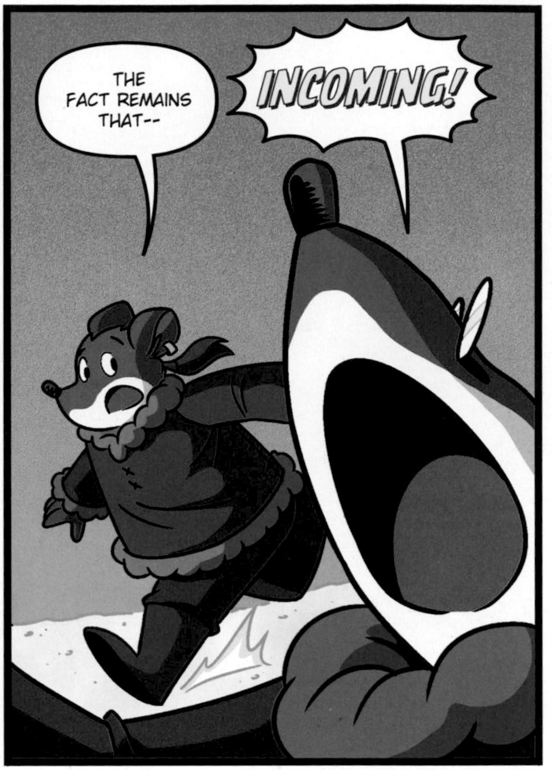
THE FACT REMAINS THAT--
INCOMING!

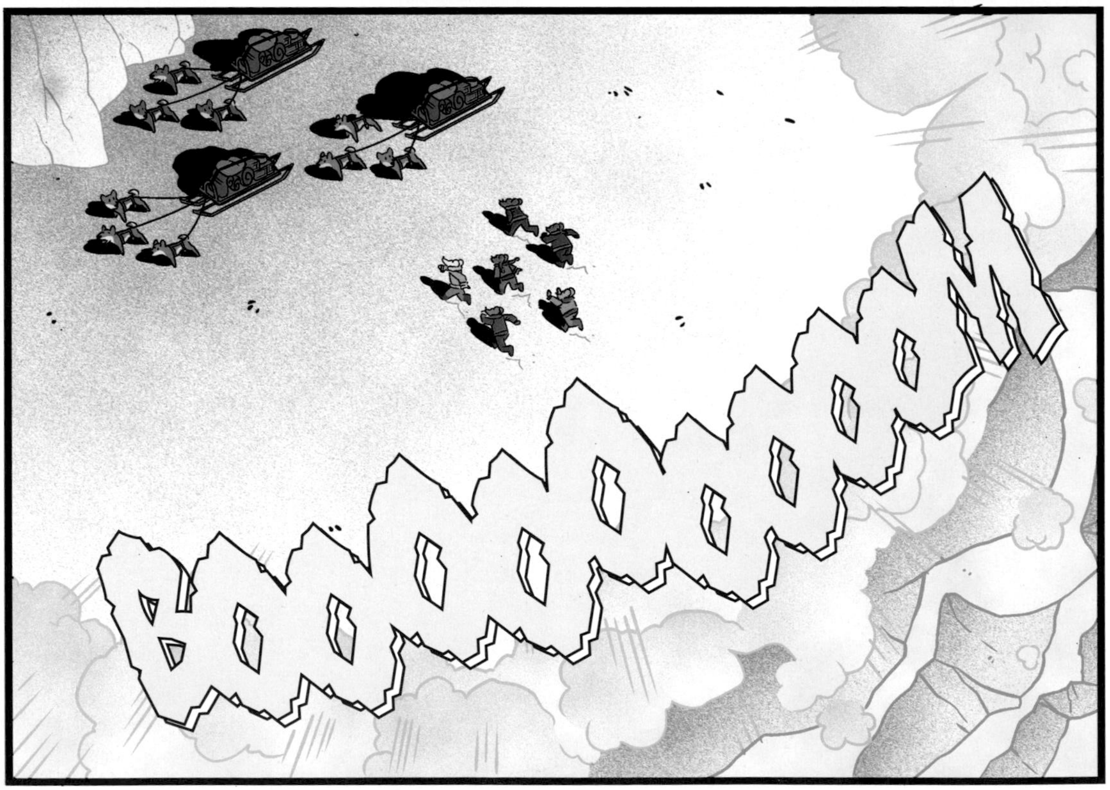
BOOOOOOOOM

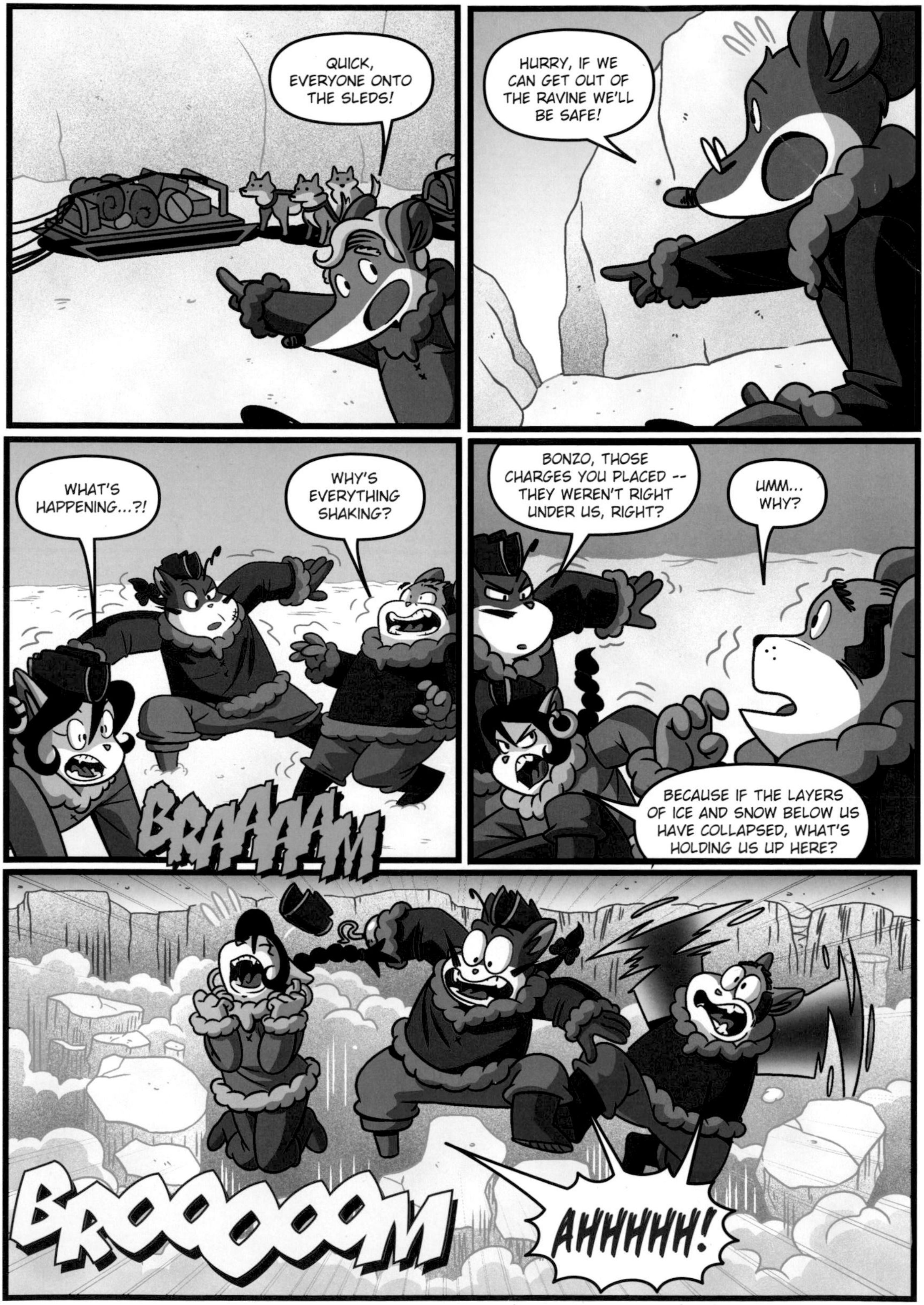
QUICK, EVERYONE ONTO THE SLEDS!
HURRY, IF WE CAN GET OUT OF THE RAVINE WE'LL BE SAFE!
WHAT'S HAPPENING...?!
WHY'S EVERYTHING SHAKING?
BRAAAAM
BONZO, THOSE CHARGES YOU PLACED -- THEY WEREN'T RIGHT UNDER US, RIGHT?
UMM... WHY?
BECAUSE IF THE LAYERS OF ICE AND SNOW BELOW US HAVE COLLAPSED, WHAT'S HOLDING US UP HERE?
BROOOOOM
AHHHHH!

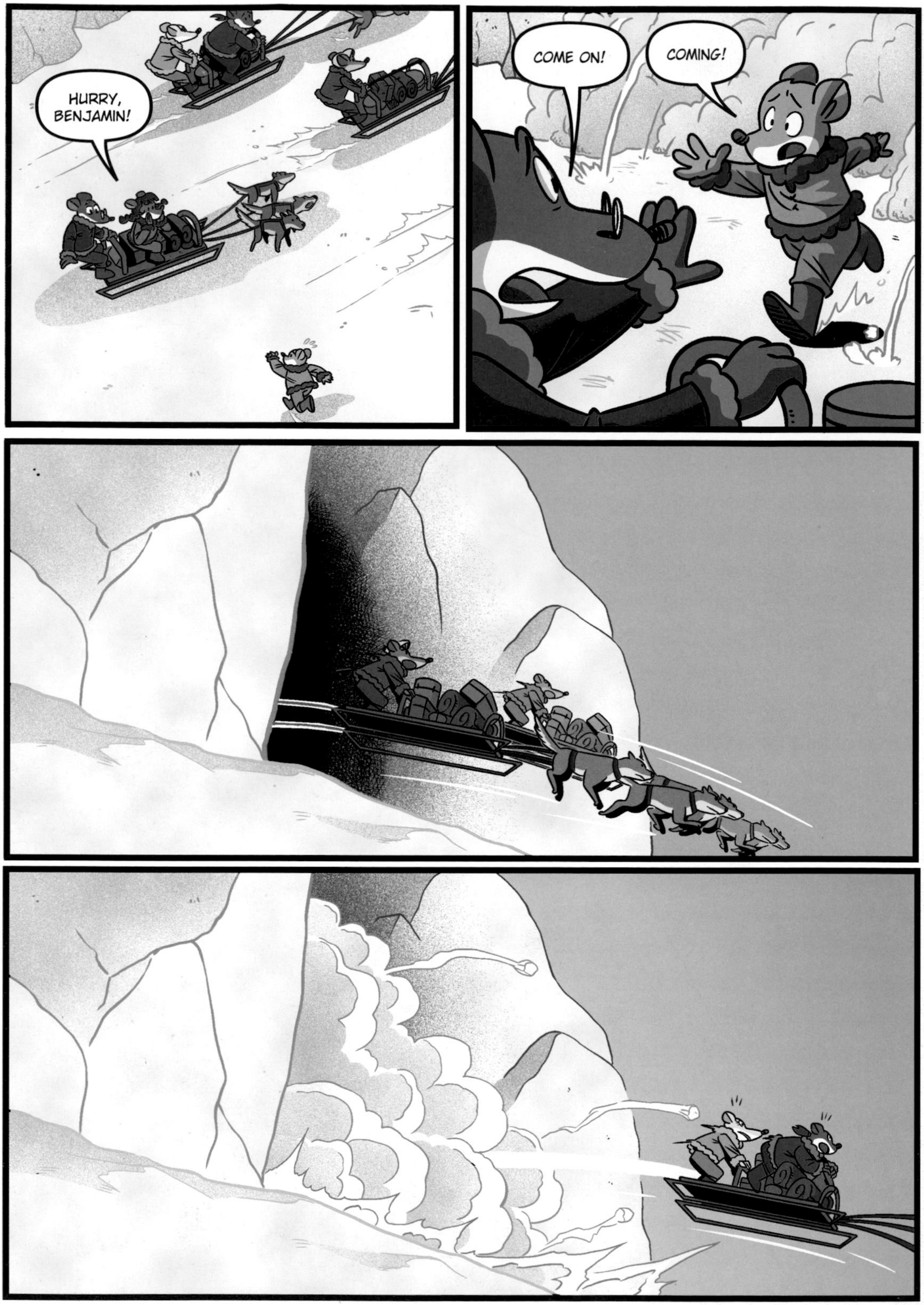
HURRY, BENJAMIN!
COME ON!
COMING!

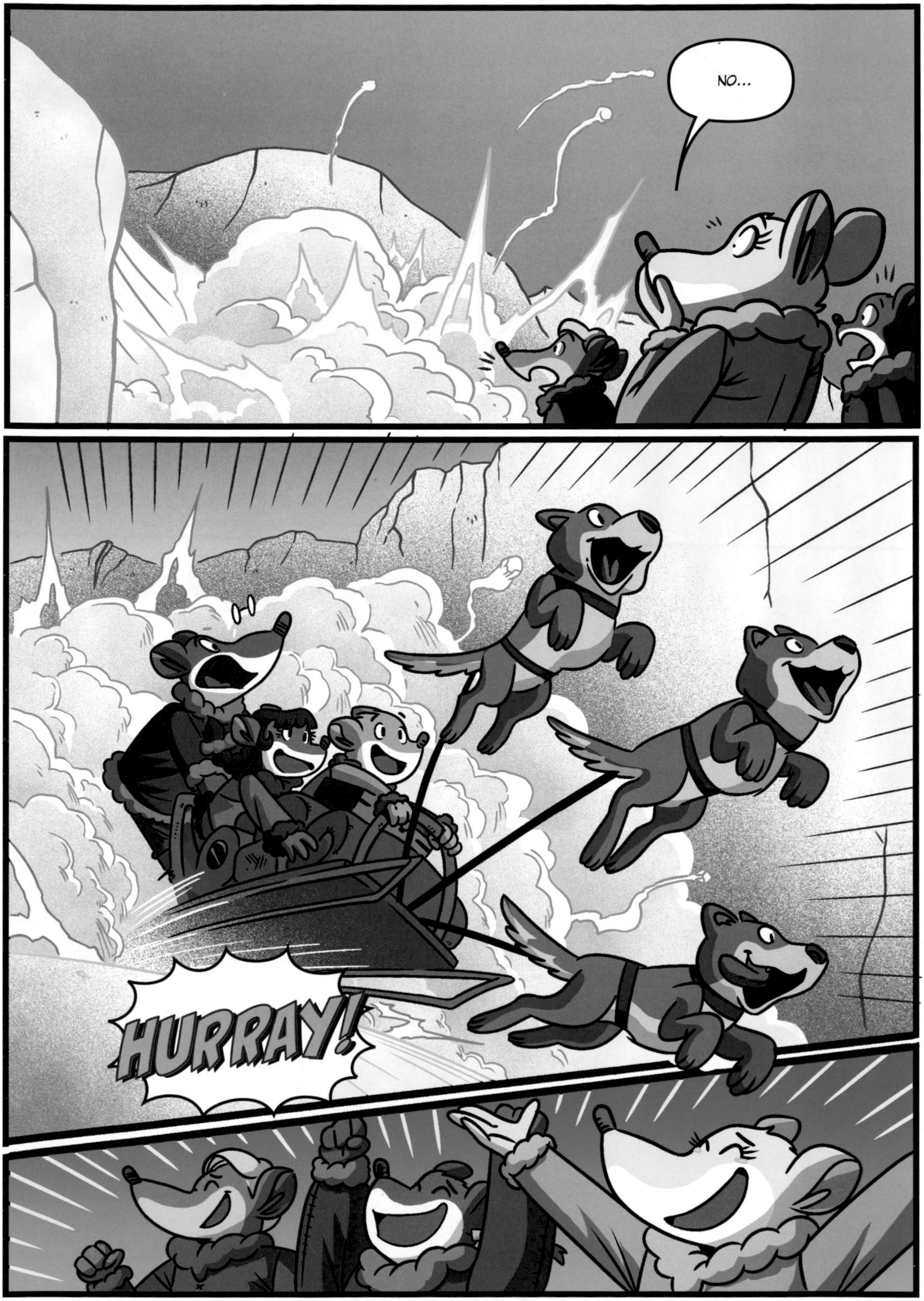
NO...
HURRAY!

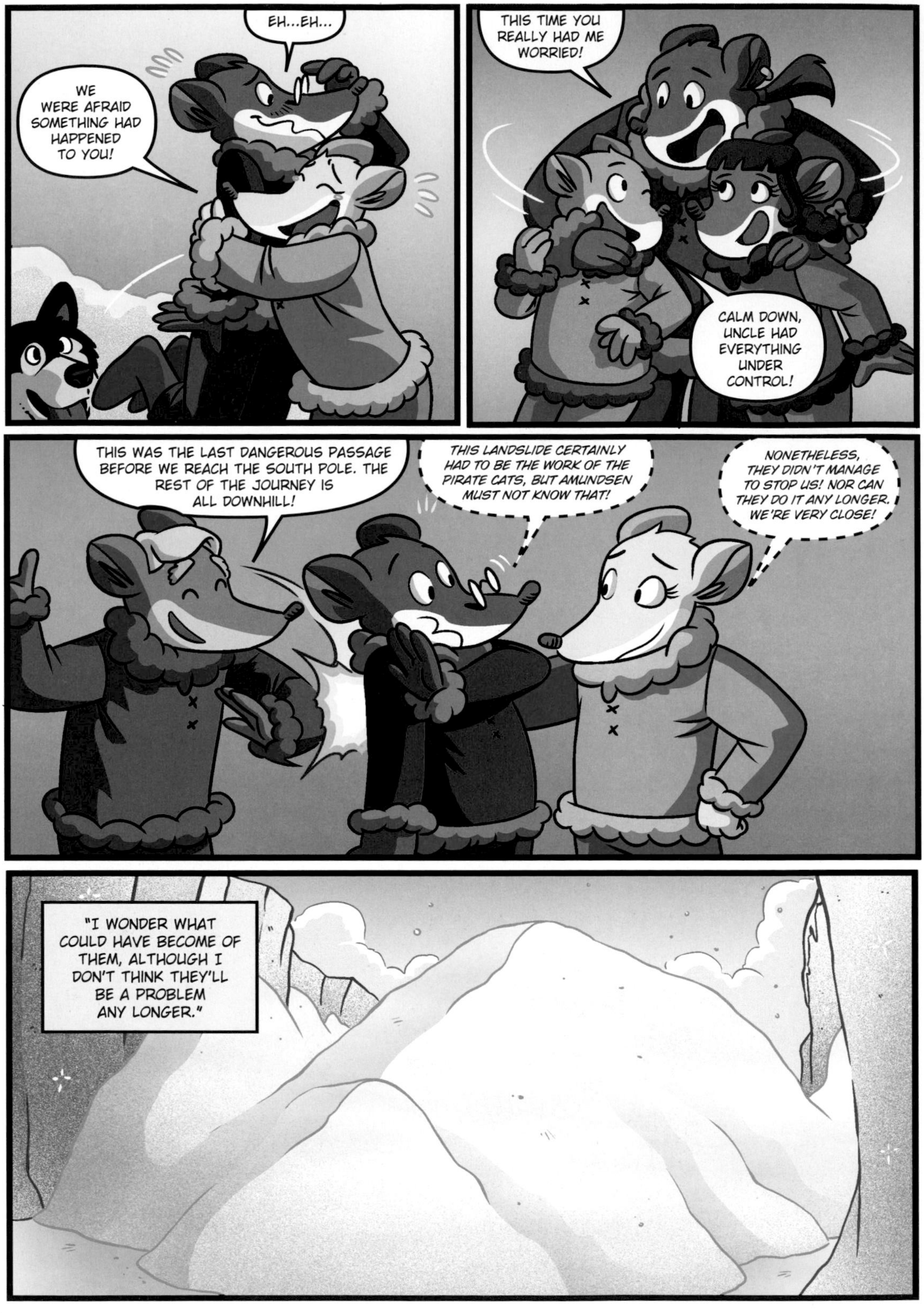
EH...EH...
WE WERE AFRAID SOMETHING HAD HAPPENED TO YOU!
THIS TIME YOU REALLY HAD ME WORRIED!
CALM DOWN, UNCLE HAD EVERYTHING UNDER CONTROL!
THIS WAS THE LAST DANGEROUS PASSAGE BEFORE WE REACH THE SOUTH POLE. THE REST OF THE JOURNEY IS ALL DOWNHILL!
THIS LANDSLIDE CERTAINLY HAD TO BE THE WORK OF THE PIRATE CATS, BUT AMUNDSEN MUST NOT KNOW THAT!
NONETHELESS, THEY DIDN'T MANAGE TO STOP US! NOR CAN THEY DO IT ANY LONGER. WE'RE VERY CLOSE!
"I WONDER WHAT COULD HAVE BECOME OF THEM, ALTHOUGH I DON'T THINK THEY'LL BE A PROBLEM ANY LONGER."

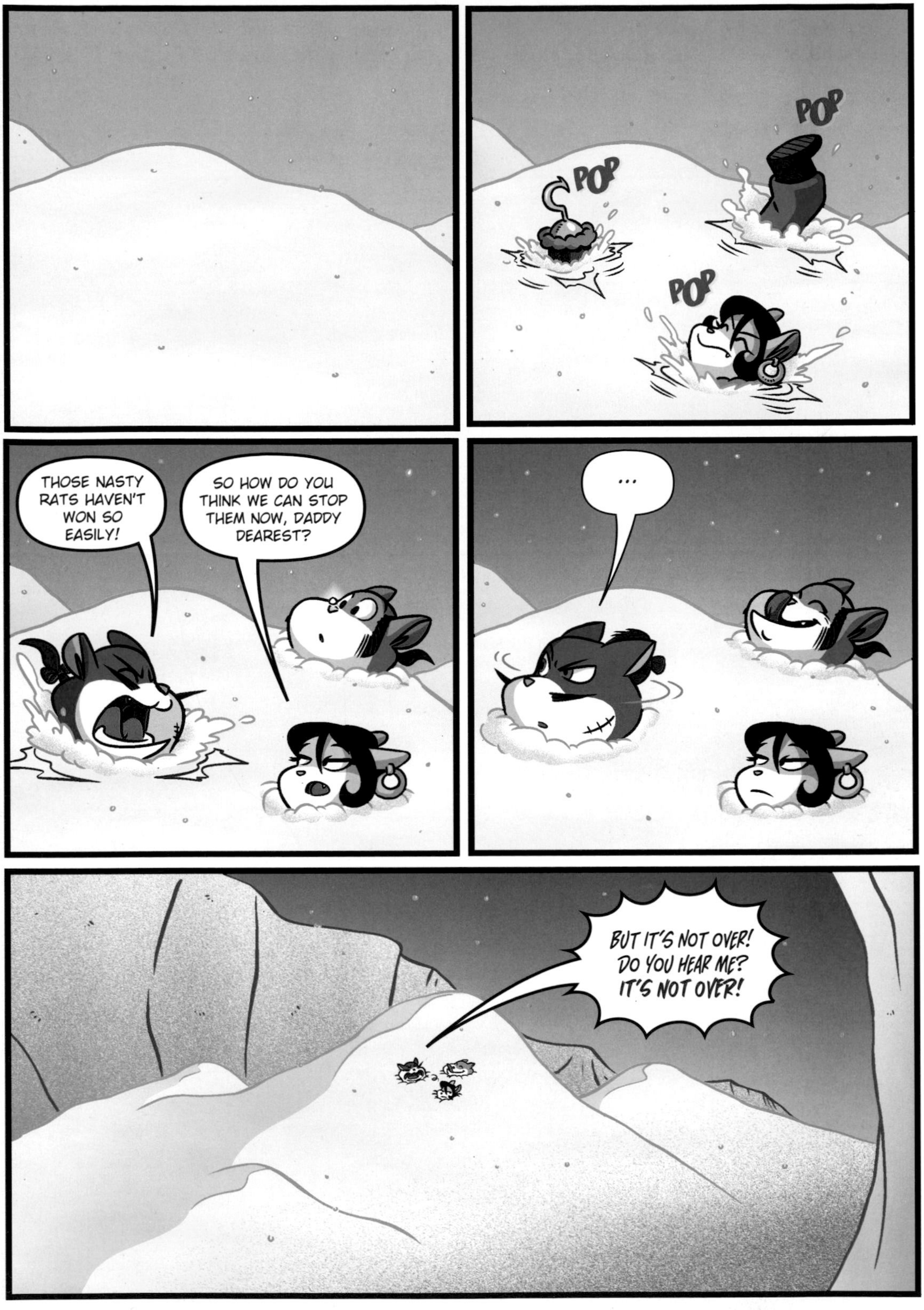
POP
POP
POP
THOSE NASTY RATS HAVEN'T WON SO EASILY!
SO HOW DO YOU THINK WE CAN STOP THEM NOW, DADDY DEAREST?
...
BUT IT'S NOT OVER! DO YOU HEAR ME? IT'S NOT OVER!

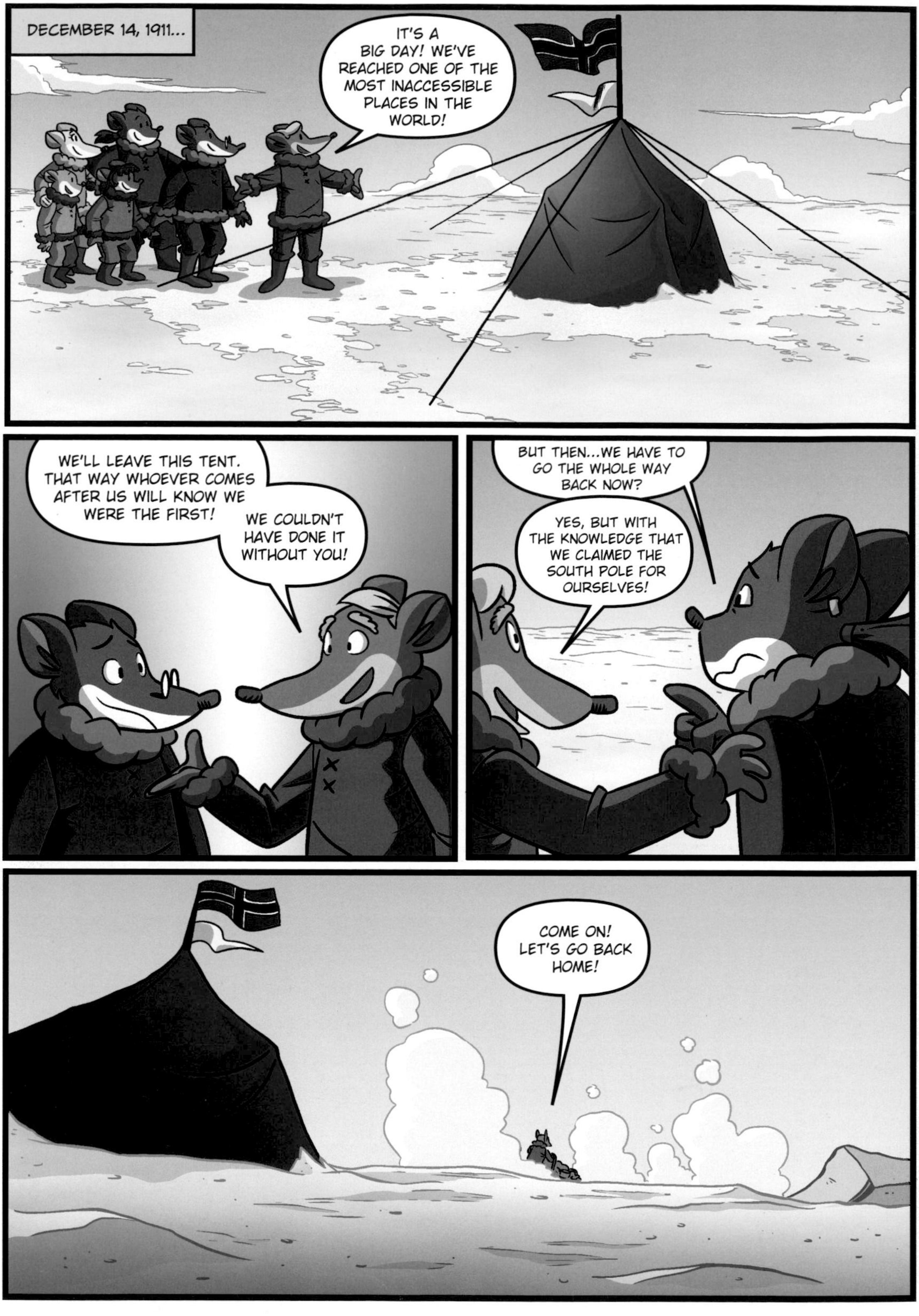
DECEMBER 14, 1911...
IT'S A BIG DAY! WE'VE REACHED ONE OF THE MOST INACCESSIBLE PLACES IN THE WORLD!
WE'LL LEAVE THIS TENT. THAT WAY WHOEVER COMES AFTER US WILL KNOW WE WERE THE FIRST!
WE COULDN'T HAVE DONE IT WITHOUT YOU!
BUT THEN...WE HAVE TO GO THE WHOLE WAY BACK NOW?
YES, BUT WITH THE KNOWLEDGE THAT WE CLAIMED THE SOUTH POLE FOR OURSELVES!
COME ON! LET'S GO BACK HOME!

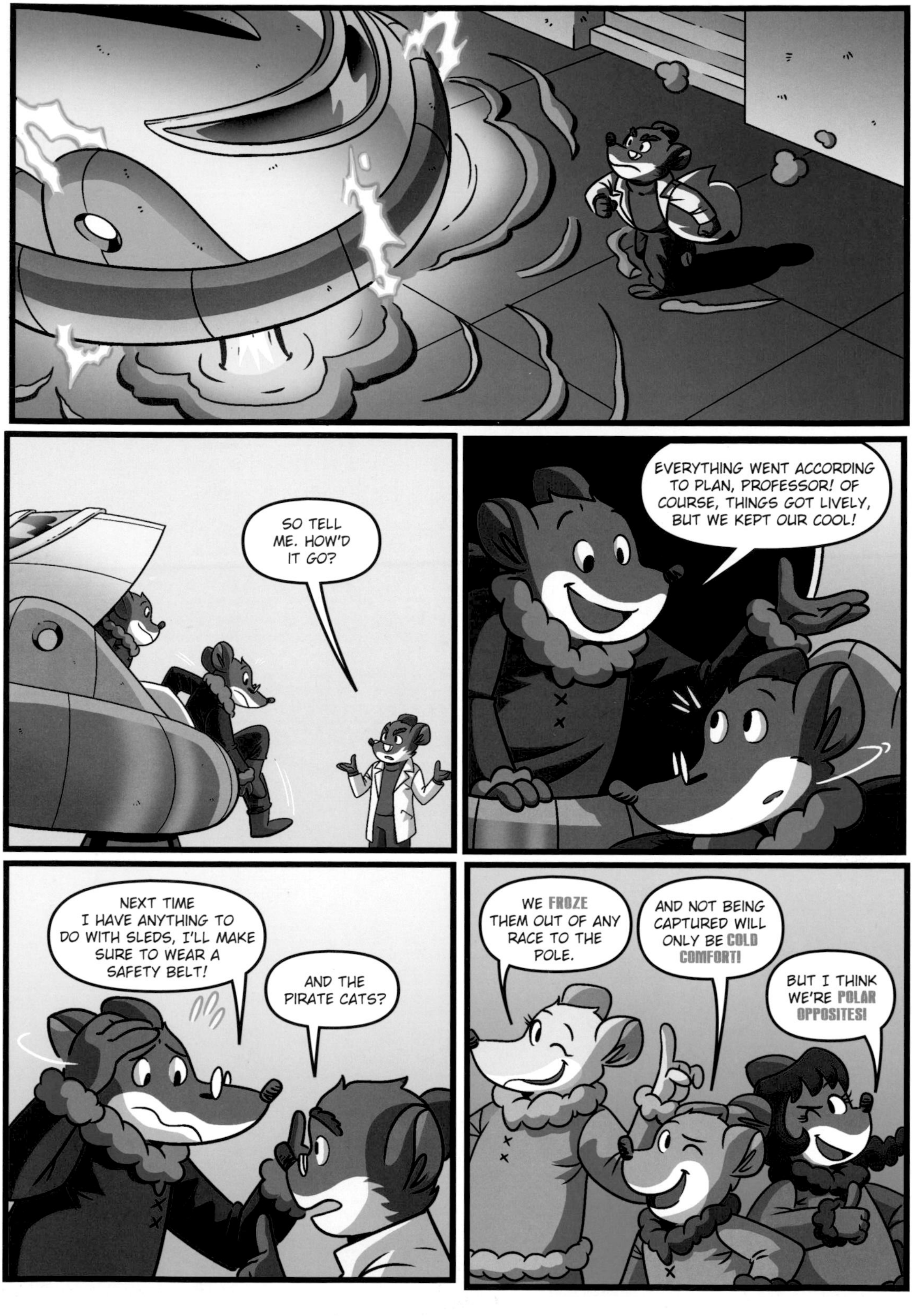
SO TELL ME. HOW'D IT GO?
EVERYTHING WENT ACCORDING TO PLAN, PROFESSOR! OF COURSE, THINGS GOT LIVELY, BUT WE KEPT OUR COOL!
NEXT TIME I HAVE ANYTHING TO DO WITH SLEDS, I'LL MAKE SURE TO WEAR A SAFETY BELT!
AND THE PIRATE CATS?
WE FROZE THEM OUT OF ANY RACE TO THE POLE.
AND NOT BEING CAPTURED WILL ONLY BE COLD COMFORT!
BUT I THINK WE'RE POLAR OPPOSITES!

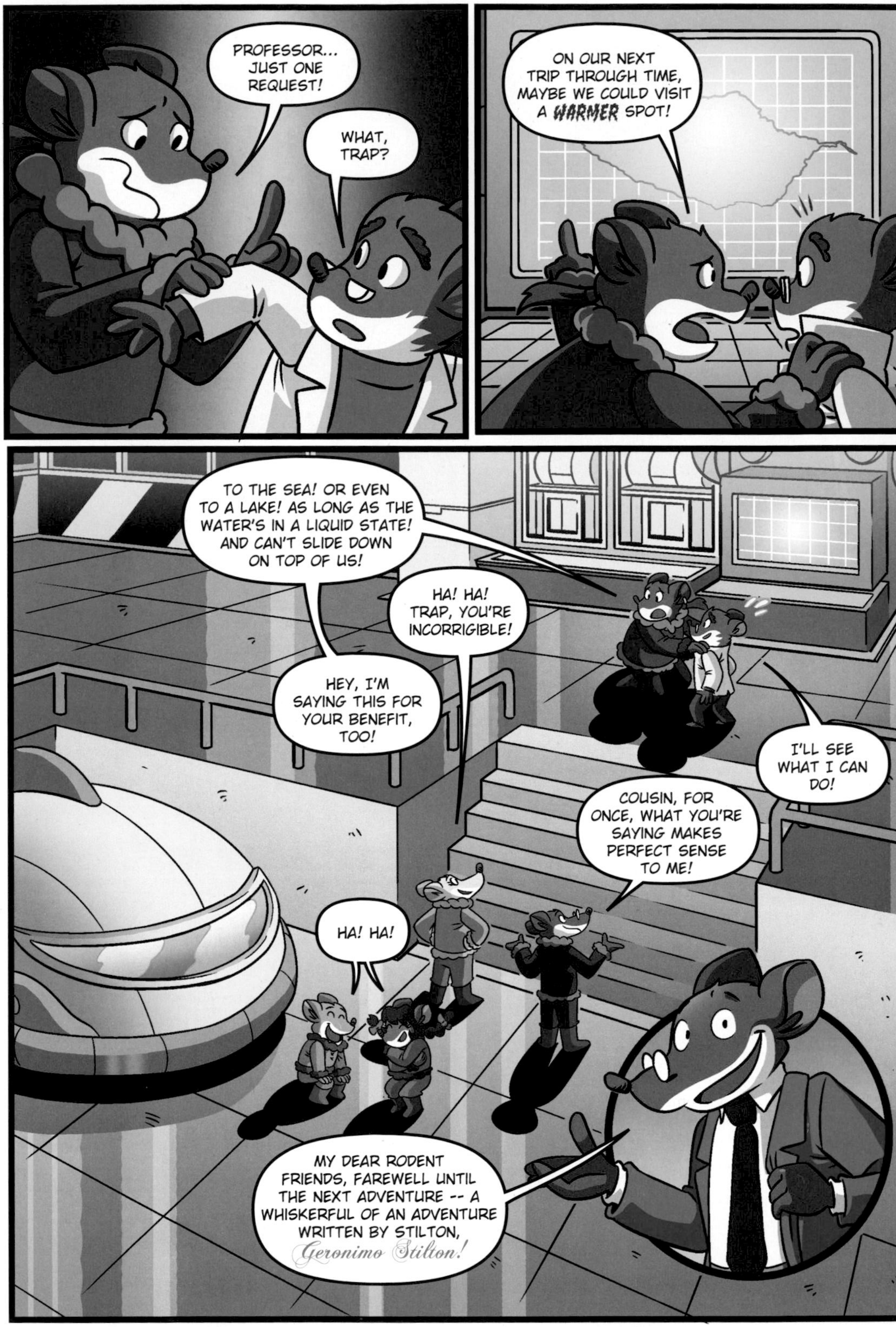
PROFESSOR... JUST ONE REQUEST!
WHAT, TRAP?
ON OUR NEXT TRIP THROUGH TIME, MAYBE WE COULD VISIT A WARMER SPOT!
TO THE SEA! OR EVEN TO A LAKE! AS LONG AS THE WATER'S IN A LIQUID STATE! AND CAN'T SLIDE DOWN ON TOP OF US!
HA! HA! TRAP, YOU'RE INCORRIGIBLE!
HEY, I'M SAYING THIS FOR YOUR BENEFIT, TOO!
I'LL SEE WHAT I CAN DO!
COUSIN, FOR ONCE, WHAT YOU'RE SAYING MAKES PERFECT SENSE TO ME!
HA! HA!
MY DEAR RODENT FRIENDS, FAREWELL UNTIL THE NEXT ADVENTURE -- A WHISKERFUL OF AN ADVENTURE WRITTEN BY STILTON, Geronimo Stilton!

Watch Out For PAPERCUTZ™

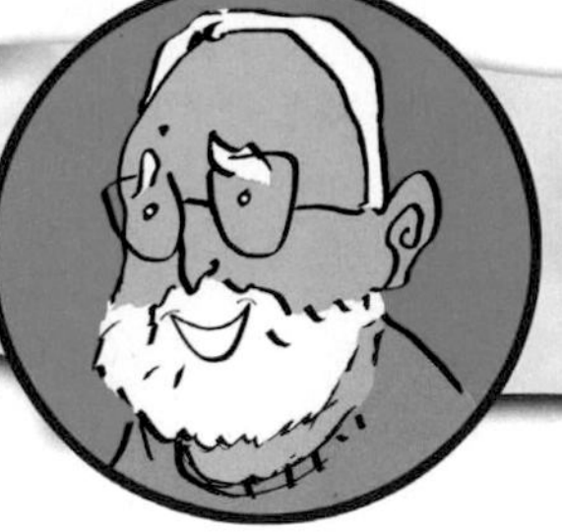

Welcome to the extra-exciting, exploration-filled, eighteenth GERONIMO STILTON graphic novel. Written by the Italian dynamic duo of Leonardo Favia and Francesco Savino, and illustrated by homeboy Ryan Jampole, all from Papercutz, those furry folks dedicated to publishing great graphic novels for all ages. I'm Salicrup, *Jim Salicrup*, the Editor-in-Chief and GPS-challenged explorer of life.

If you've visited geronimostilton.com recently, you may have seen that there's a section devoted to *The Philosophy of Geronimo Stilton*. We liked what we saw so much that we'd like to share a little bit of it right here, starting with…

GERONIMO STILTON AND HIS MOTIVATIONS

The weaknesses of Geronimo Stilton make him even more likeable; you feel sorry for him, you laugh with him and you celebrate with him at the end, because all his defeats become successes. With his actions and his ability to laugh at himself, Geronimo Stilton conveys ever-present values: the importance of family, the capacity to overcome your fears, the acceptance of other people's faults, the importance of education, consistency, approachability, open mindedness towards other cultures, curiosity about what you don't know, the knowledge that teamwork is more successful than acting as an individual, world peace, friendship, love, solidarity, honesty, loyalty, sincerity, and respect for the elderly and those with lesser abilities.

And that's just the beginning! There's a lot more and we invite you to go to geronimostilton.com to check it out for yourself. But let's just take another look at that first sentence, shall we? "The weaknesses of Geronimo Stilton make him even more likeable." That may sound a little strange to you at first, as don't we all try to avoid having any weaknesses? Yet, depending on what we decide to focus on in life, we can't all be great at everything, can we? We're constantly trying to be our very best, but just to do well at a few things usually means not doing all sorts of other things. For example, Geronimo is a great editor, but as he tells Trap, "the paper had assigned me to report on the big game, but it wasn't one of the easiest jobs for me, given that I'm not a very sporty man, or rather, mouse." Geronimo's aware of his limitations, but he doesn't let that stop him from doing his job. (Let's assume that after Geronimo and his fellow travelers returned to Professor von Volt's lab, he then raced back to the football stadium to continue reporting on the Cheese Bowl!)

Weaknesses are nothing to be ashamed about. We all have our own individual strengths and weaknesses and it's up to us to make the best of it. Look at how Geronimo freely admits that he doesn't know a lot about sports. That's a much better approach to take than being ashamed and pretending he's an expert on the subject. By being honest people, and mice, we can understand that he's trying his best to understand something that he's not very knowledgeable about. When you act this way, more often than not, people will try to help you, and explain everything to you. Sure, there will be those who might actually tease you, but how much harm can they do when you've already said that you don't know much about something? Look what happened to Geronimo— he revealed his weakness, and within minutes he scored a touchdown in the big game! Sure that sounds far-fetched, but as an editor myself, and not "a very sporty man," I've always found it better to give it my best shot, rather than run away and hide.

Years ago, I was invited to play volleyball with my co-workers. I had never played that game before, or much sports in general, but I agreed and did my best. And guess what? I was terrible! Just awful! I was the worst player on the team by far. But I kept playing, week after week, and while I never became a good player—I did get better. And after a few months, people would tell me that they were impressed with how much better I started to play. Well, I couldn't have gotten any worse! But just as Geronimo's weaknesses make him likeable, mine also helped people like me, and also respect me for my willingness to fail and keep on trying.

And if I can share a little bit of my philosophy, I think that's a big part of what life is about. Not being afraid to fail, and always trying your best. You may not always succeed, but you will learn a lot, and people will like and respect you.

Gee, and all that was just based on the first sentence of *The Philosophy of Geronimo Stilton*!

On the following pages, enjoy a special preview of THEA STILTON #6 "The Thea Sisters and the Mystery at Sea." It's available at booksellers now, and it sure looks like the Thea Sisters also embrace Geronimo's philosophy as they once again work together to help the environment.

See you in the future! Jim

STAY IN TOUCH!

EMAIL:	salicrup@papercutz.com
WEB:	papercutz.com
TWITTER:	@papercutzgn
FACEBOOK:	PAPERCUTZGRAPHICNOVELS
FAN MAIL:	Papercutz, 160 Broadway, Suite 700, East Wing, New York, NY 10038

Special Preview of THEA STILTON #6 "The Thea Sisters and the Mystery at Sea"!

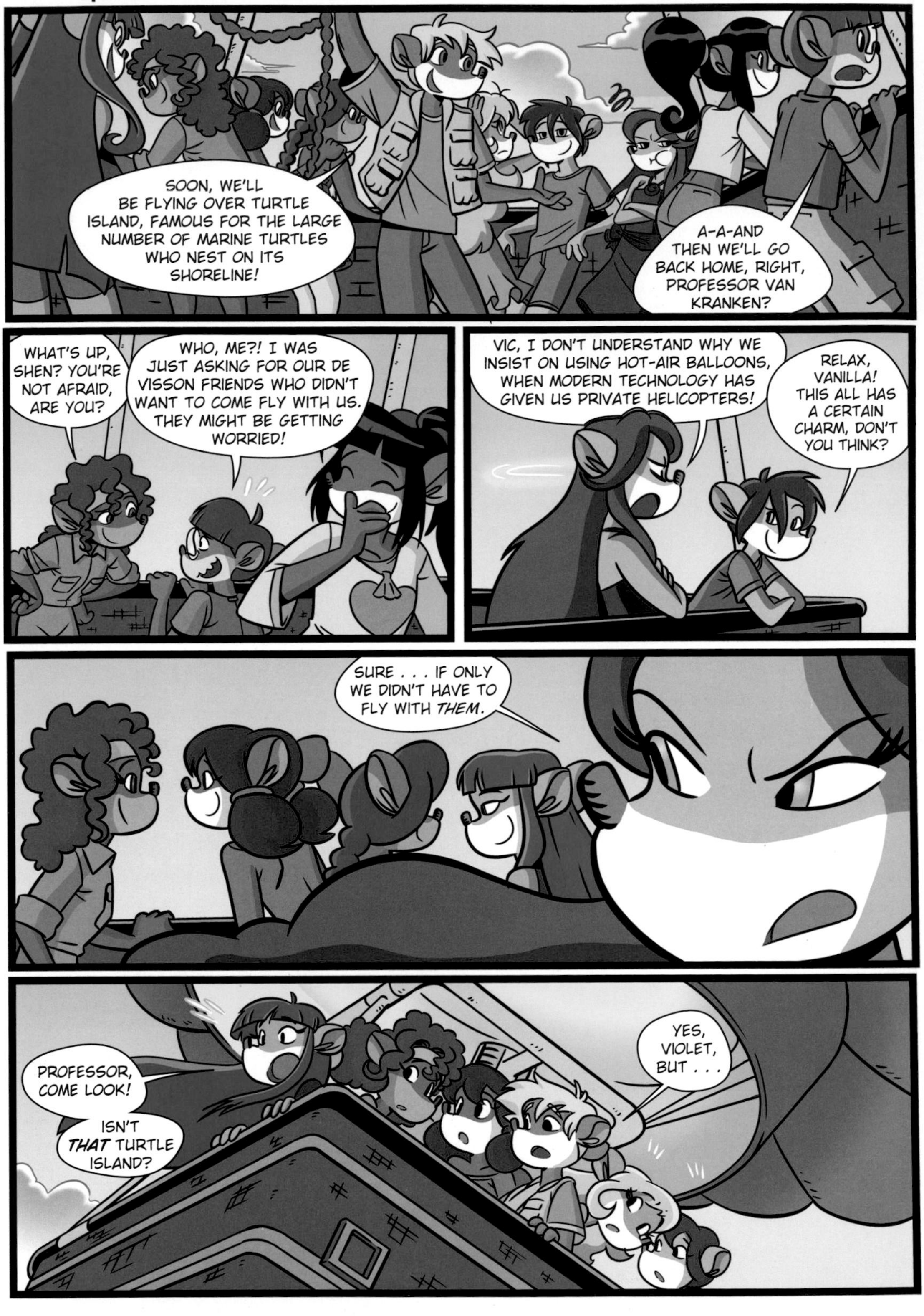
SOON, WE'LL BE FLYING OVER TURTLE ISLAND, FAMOUS FOR THE LARGE NUMBER OF MARINE TURTLES WHO NEST ON ITS SHORELINE!
A-A-AND THEN WE'LL GO BACK HOME, RIGHT, PROFESSOR VAN KRANKEN?
WHAT'S UP, SHEN? YOU'RE NOT AFRAID, ARE YOU?
WHO, ME?! I WAS JUST ASKING FOR OUR DE VISSON FRIENDS WHO DIDN'T WANT TO COME FLY WITH US. THEY MIGHT BE GETTING WORRIED!
VIC, I DON'T UNDERSTAND WHY WE INSIST ON USING HOT-AIR BALLOONS, WHEN MODERN TECHNOLOGY HAS GIVEN US PRIVATE HELICOPTERS!
RELAX, VANILLA! THIS ALL HAS A CERTAIN CHARM, DON'T YOU THINK?
SURE . . . IF ONLY WE DIDN'T HAVE TO FLY WITH *THEM*.
PROFESSOR, COME LOOK!
ISN'T *THAT* TURTLE ISLAND?
YES, VIOLET, BUT . . .

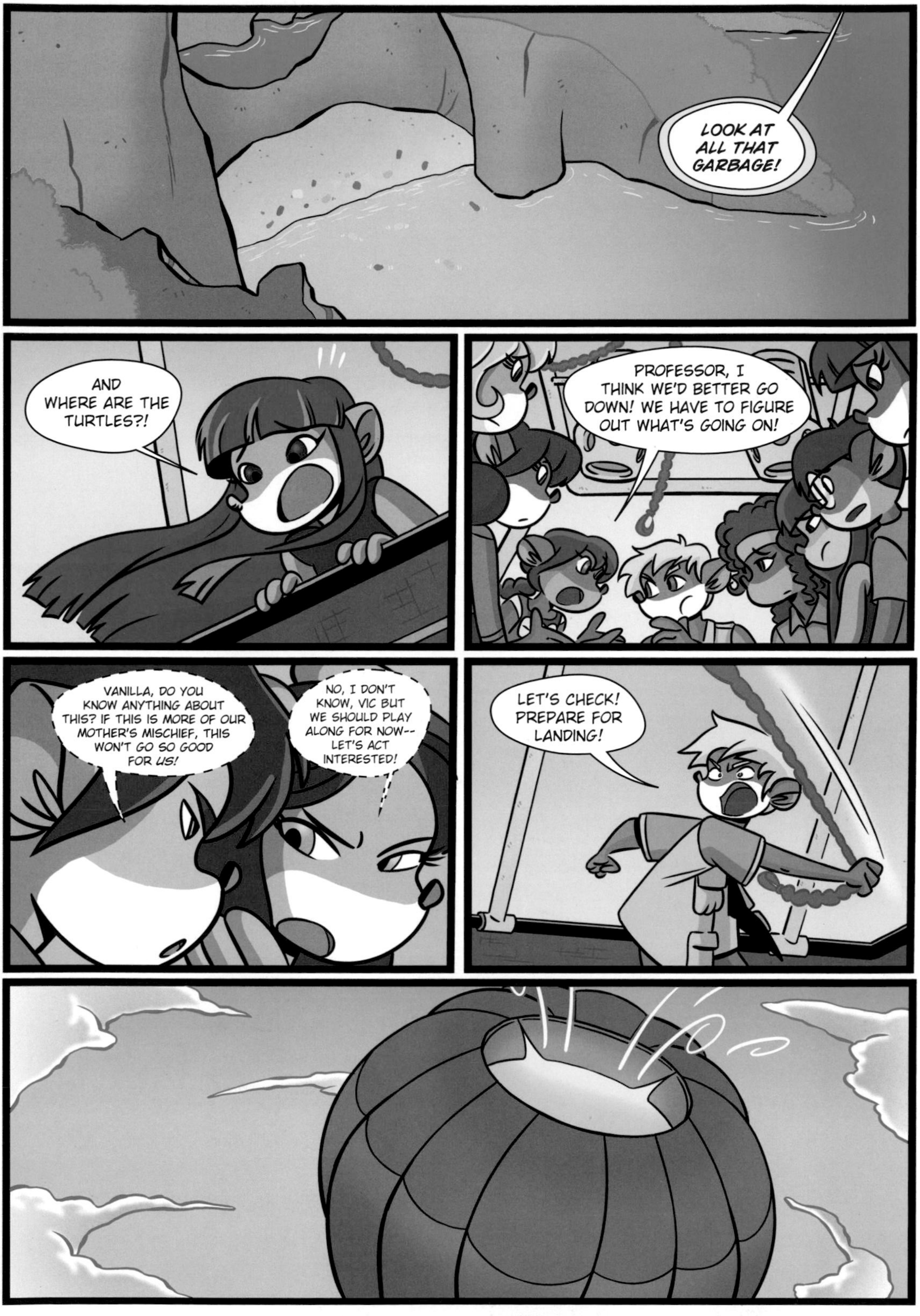
LOOK AT ALL THAT GARBAGE!
AND WHERE ARE THE TURTLES?!
PROFESSOR, I THINK WE'D BETTER GO DOWN! WE HAVE TO FIGURE OUT WHAT'S GOING ON!
VANILLA, DO YOU KNOW ANYTHING ABOUT THIS? IF THIS IS MORE OF OUR MOTHER'S MISCHIEF, THIS WON'T GO SO GOOD FOR US!
NO, I DON'T KNOW, VIC BUT WE SHOULD PLAY ALONG FOR NOW-- LET'S ACT INTERESTED!
LET'S CHECK! PREPARE FOR LANDING!

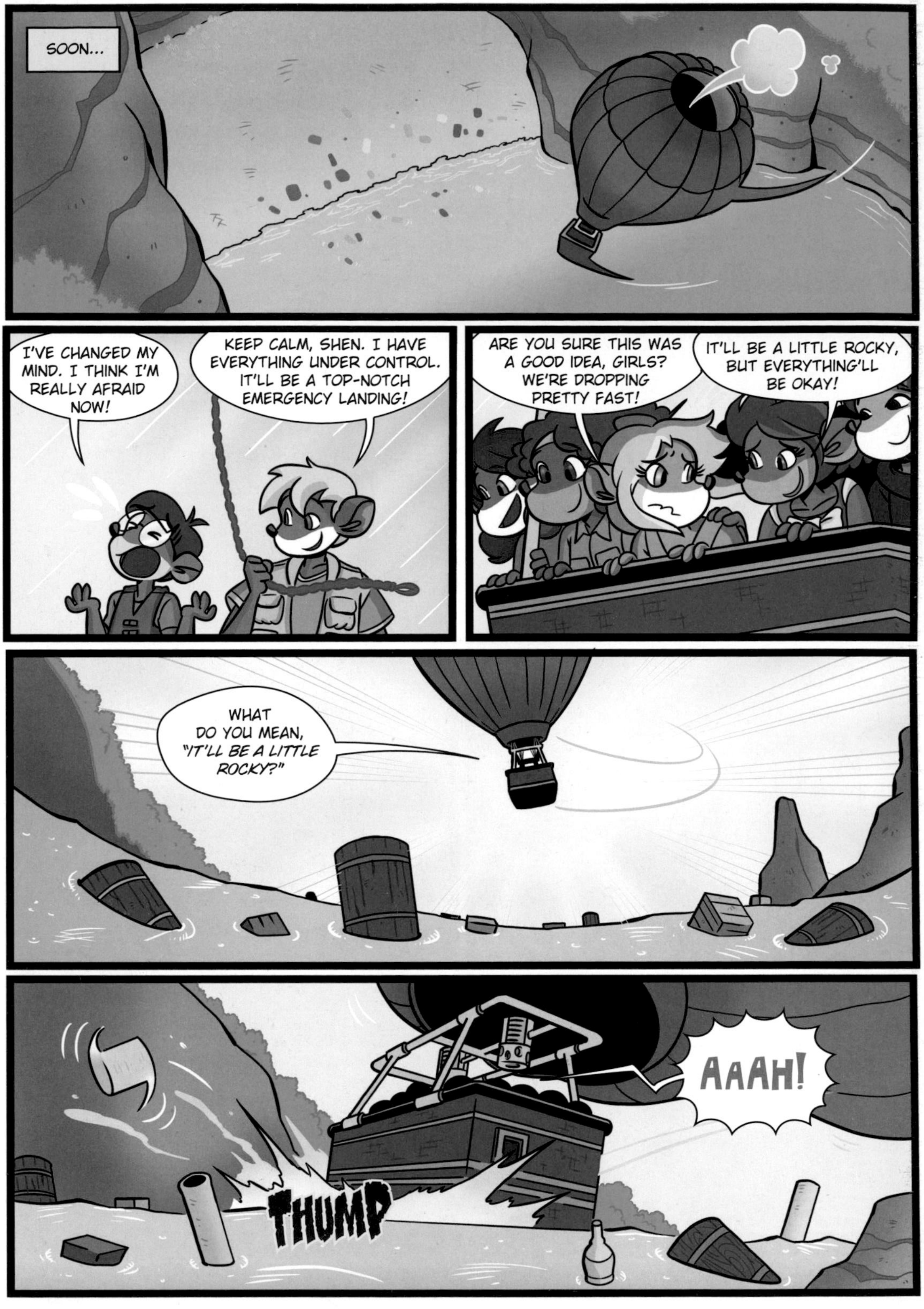
SOON...
I'VE CHANGED MY MIND. I THINK I'M REALLY AFRAID NOW!
KEEP CALM, SHEN. I HAVE EVERYTHING UNDER CONTROL. IT'LL BE A TOP-NOTCH EMERGENCY LANDING!
ARE YOU SURE THIS WAS A GOOD IDEA, GIRLS? WE'RE DROPPING PRETTY FAST!
IT'LL BE A LITTLE ROCKY, BUT EVERYTHING'LL BE OKAY!
WHAT DO YOU MEAN, *"IT'LL BE A LITTLE ROCKY?"*
AAAH!
THUMP

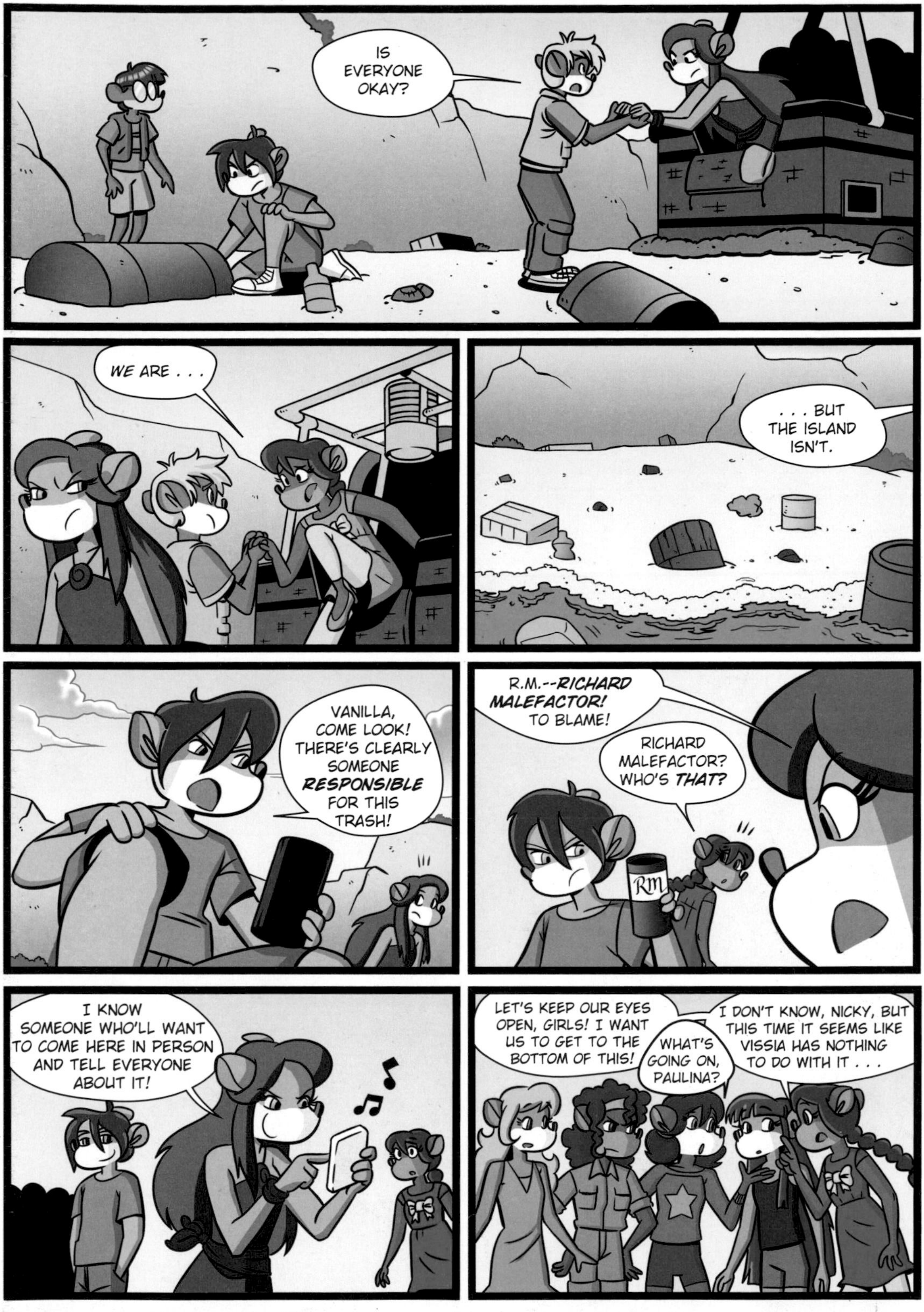
IS EVERYONE OKAY?
WE ARE . . .
. . . BUT THE ISLAND ISN'T.
VANILLA, COME LOOK! THERE'S CLEARLY SOMEONE RESPONSIBLE FOR THIS TRASH!
R.M.--RICHARD MALEFACTOR! TO BLAME!
RICHARD MALEFACTOR? WHO'S THAT?
RM
I KNOW SOMEONE WHO'LL WANT TO COME HERE IN PERSON AND TELL EVERYONE ABOUT IT!
LET'S KEEP OUR EYES OPEN, GIRLS! I WANT US TO GET TO THE BOTTOM OF THIS!
WHAT'S GOING ON, PAULINA?
I DON'T KNOW, NICKY, BUT THIS TIME IT SEEMS LIKE VISSIA HAS NOTHING TO DO WITH IT . . .

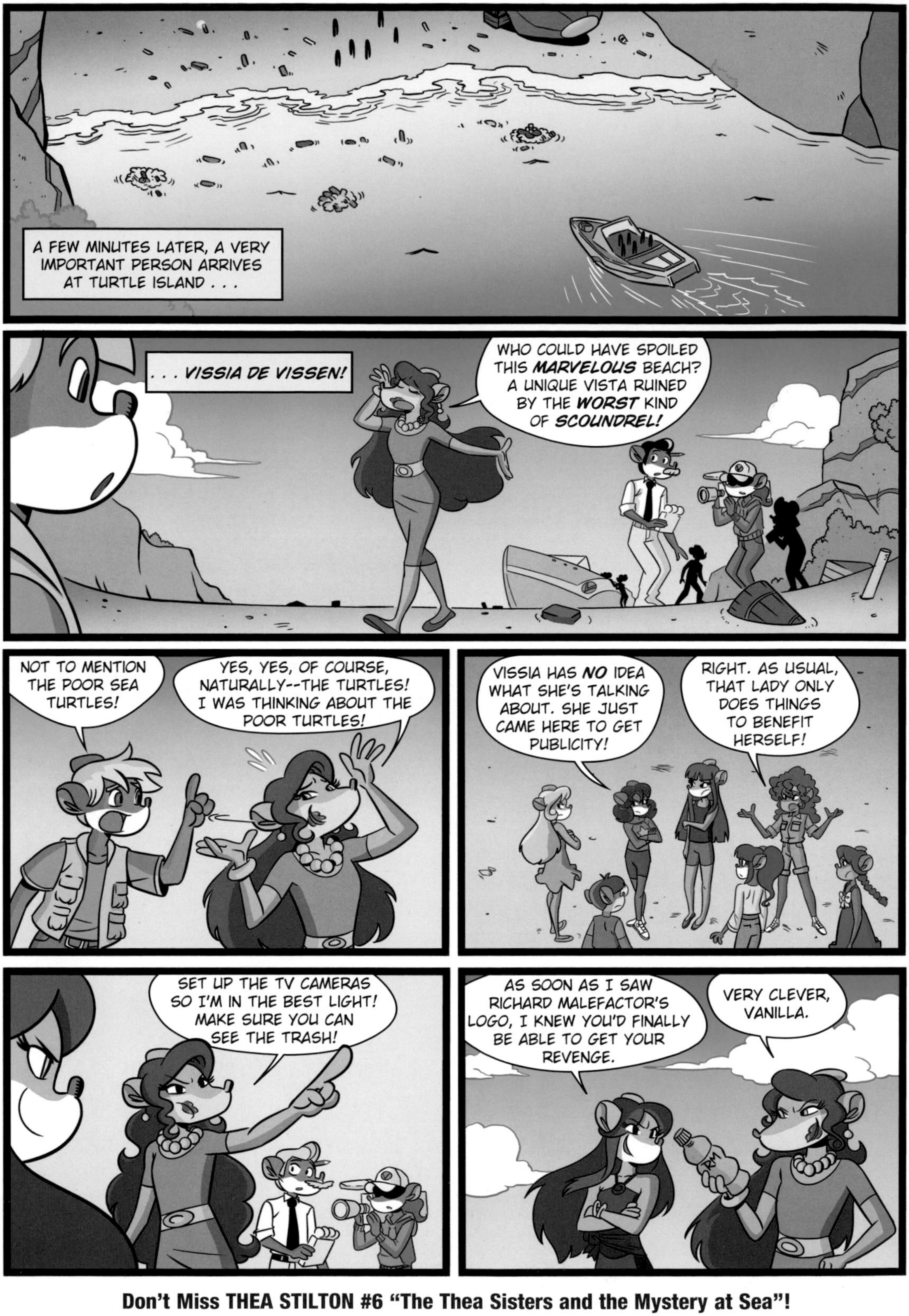
A FEW MINUTES LATER, A VERY IMPORTANT PERSON ARRIVES AT TURTLE ISLAND . . .
. . . VISSIA DE VISSEN!
WHO COULD HAVE SPOILED THIS MARVELOUS BEACH? A UNIQUE VISTA RUINED BY THE WORST KIND OF SCOUNDREL!
NOT TO MENTION THE POOR SEA TURTLES!
YES, YES, OF COURSE, NATURALLY--THE TURTLES! I WAS THINKING ABOUT THE POOR TURTLES!
VISSIA HAS NO IDEA WHAT SHE'S TALKING ABOUT. SHE JUST CAME HERE TO GET PUBLICITY!
RIGHT. AS USUAL, THAT LADY ONLY DOES THINGS TO BENEFIT HERSELF!
SET UP THE TV CAMERAS SO I'M IN THE BEST LIGHT! MAKE SURE YOU CAN SEE THE TRASH!
AS SOON AS I SAW RICHARD MALEFACTOR'S LOGO, I KNEW YOU'D FINALLY BE ABLE TO GET YOUR REVENGE.
VERY CLEVER, VANILLA.

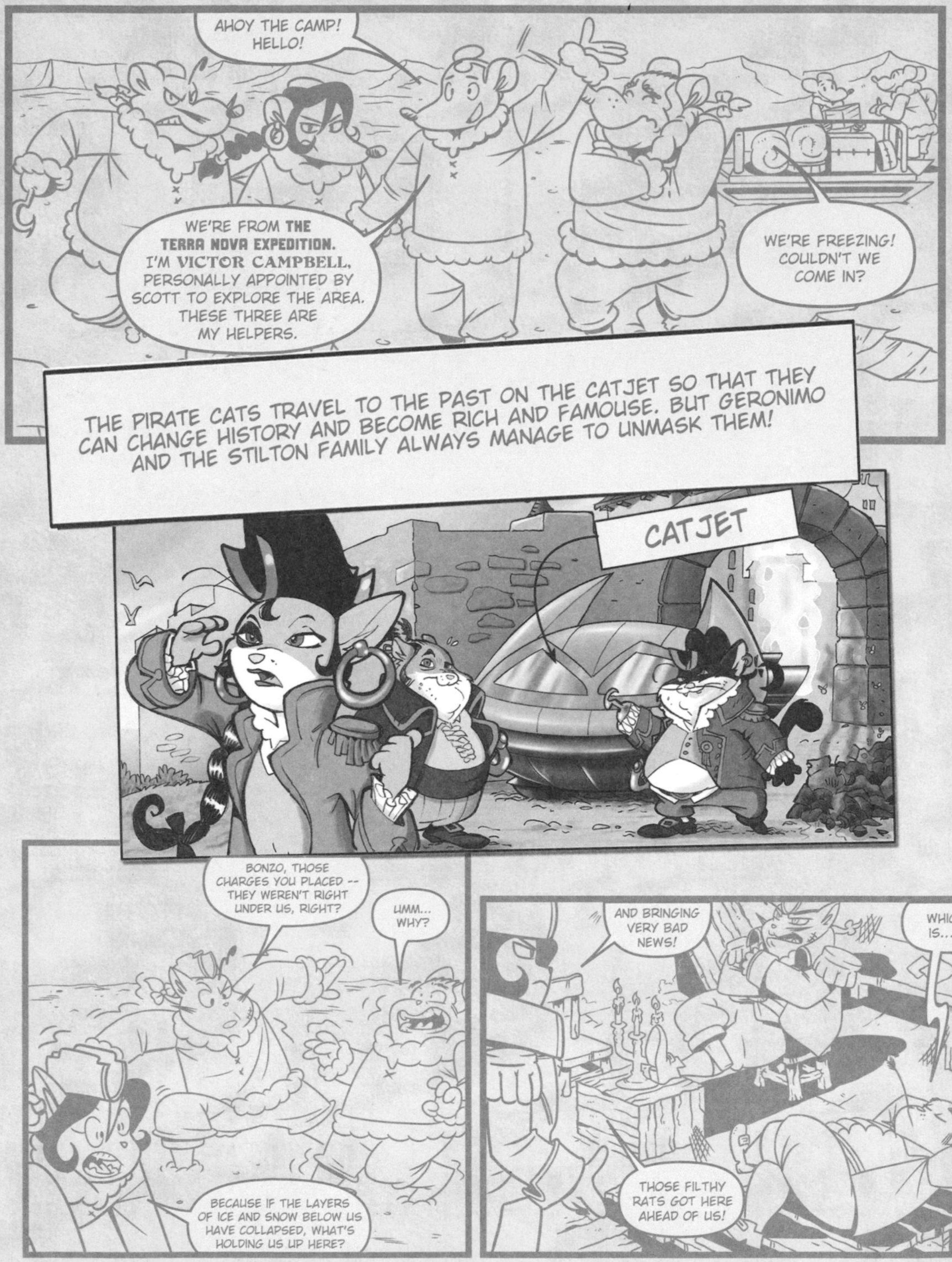
AHOY THE CAMP! HELLO!
WE'RE FROM THE TERRA NOVA EXPEDITION. I'M VICTOR CAMPBELL, PERSONALLY APPOINTED BY SCOTT TO EXPLORE THE AREA. THESE THREE ARE MY HELPERS.
WE'RE FREEZING! COULDN'T WE COME IN?
THE PIRATE CATS TRAVEL TO THE PAST ON THE CATJET SO THAT THEY CAN CHANGE HISTORY AND BECOME RICH AND FAMOUSE. BUT GERONIMO AND THE STILTON FAMILY ALWAYS MANAGE TO UNMASK THEM!
CATJET
BONZO, THOSE CHARGES YOU PLACED -- THEY WEREN'T RIGHT UNDER US, RIGHT?
UMM... WHY?
BECAUSE IF THE LAYERS OF ICE AND SNOW BELOW US HAVE COLLAPSED, WHAT'S HOLDING US UP HERE?
AND BRINGING VERY BAD NEWS!
WHICH IS...?
THOSE FILTHY RATS GOT HERE AHEAD OF US!